READY FOR HER YETI

ALASKA YETI SERIES
BOOK 1

NEVA POST

ICICLE INK, LLC

Editing: Elizabeth Grover, Kathryn Schieber of BFF Editing, and Missy Borucki

Cover Design: MiblArt

ISBN: 978-1-958830-02-4

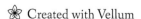 Created with Vellum

For Scott, my yeti.

Can beauty love the snow beast?

Helen is eager for a break from her life after being dumped before her wedding. She jumps at the chance to return to Alaska as a winter caretaker at a resort lodge. A month of solitude is exactly what she needs to recharge, refocus, and regain control of her life. But Helen discovers she isn't alone. The position has already been filled by the legendary yeti, who turns out to be kind, quirky, and hot enough to melt snow.

Rab is ready to hunker down for winter and enjoy some creature comforts. He has food in the pantry, stacks of firewood, and a bed with sheets that feel like silk after months of sleeping on the ground. There's only one problem. The elusive beauty who secretly stole his heart years ago is back and has claimed his job. He never dared reveal himself to Helen before, but now that he has, he's afraid one month with her won't be nearly enough.

CHAPTER ONE

Rab relaxed against the side of the hot tub, watching through slitted eyes as fluffy snowflakes drifted lazily through the air. Some melted into the water churning around him, some collected on his thick, white fur. His eyes drifted closed, and he sighed, letting the jets work their magic on his tired muscles.

Yeti were practically impervious to the cold, but he always enjoyed a soak in an outdoor hot tub, especially in the falling snow.

The May climbing season in the Alaska Range was rad, but October had its own charms. It meant peace, quiet, and down duvets. After a summer of rocky outcrops and butting heads with Dall sheep, the Toklat Lodge was a little piece of Shangri-la.

On a cloudless day, the full southern view from the lodge's wide deck presented massive snowy mountain peaks, including Denali, the Great One herself. Tourists traveled thousands of miles for a chance to see the view, and locals didn't take it for granted.

However, snow-filled clouds obscured the mountains today. Rab dunked his head and slicked his fur back from his face, careful not to scratch his bare cheeks with claws still jagged from summer rock climbing. His palms were calloused and coarse too, but a second shower, a pumice stone, and some moisturizer would take care of the roughest edges.

As winter caretaker, he had free rein of the empty lodge, and whatever lotions and potions the summer tourists left behind were fair game.

Water sluiced down Rab's furry body when he rose, and he grabbed his towel before stepping out of the hot tub. As he wrapped the damp towel around his waist, a distant noise caught his attention. It sounded like the whine of a plane engine. But Dale, a pilot and co-owner of the lodge, wouldn't be here until the end of the month. And Rab wasn't expecting anyone else until his friends arrived for the New Year's holiday. Nearly one-hundred miles of mountain roads, now closed and buried in snowdrifts, separated Rab from the nearest town, which was just how he liked it.

Dale was one of the few humans who knew Rab and his kind existed. Some yeti lived closer to and even overlapped the edges of human civilization, but not Rab. Dale had hired Rab to care for the Toklat Lodge in winter. In summer, Rab roamed the wild Alaska Range. And in spring, he worked as a climbing guide on Denali with Mountain High Guiding Service. They were a yeti-friendly company, though few staff knew what Rab was. He kept his blue skin and white fur hidden under white zinc oxide and bright outdoor clothing. The clients were none the wiser.

No longer hearing the plane engine, Rab headed for his room. The slate-tiled shower in the Foraker Suite was like a climate-controlled waterfall. As hot water rained over him, he grabbed a bottle of shampoo and squeezed. Soap oozed from the punctures he'd inadvertently made with his claws. The humid air filled with a fruity scent as he lathered up, rinsing the hot tub chemicals from his fur.

Before his soak, he'd showered to wash the dirt and detritus from his fur—he wasn't an animal. This second shower was mostly about self-pampering. Again, because he wasn't an animal.

He pumped a handful of conditioner from a larger bottle before spreading it over his entire fur-covered body, rubbing sore, tight muscles as he went. He'd traveled hundreds of miles on foot through the Alaska Range over the last week, and his forty-two-year-old body had the aches to prove it.

The goop smelled minty and would undoubtedly fluff up his fur, making him look like a seven-foot-tall poodle with a blowout. Whatever. No one would see him. Most people never saw Rab. A master of fading into the shadows and going unnoticed, he made sure of it. This gig as winter caretaker at a closed lodge was perfect for a yeti who occasionally appreciated the finer amenities—the creature comforts, as it were.

The drain clogged, and he scooped a handful of fur out of the cover, but it soon clogged again—inevitable after months of not taking a proper bath. He needed to give himself a good brushing outside, where the wind would carry the tufts of white fur away. Later. Right now, it was nap time. Then he'd raid the pantry and kitchen.

Rab turned the water off and grabbed two of the lodge's plush towels. After wrapping his head in one, he ran the other over his body, buffing and rubbing himself right into that fluffy poodle look. He tossed the wet towels into the hamper before going into the bedroom.

He surveyed the expanse of the California king bed, large for humans but barely adequate for a yeti. Compared to all the places and conditions in which he'd slept the last few months—hard, rocky outcrops in mild weather, and wet caves to escape gale force winds and blinding blizzards—slumbering on the soft mattress would be blissful. Last night, he'd slept in a snowy tree well. It had protected him from the weather and had been warm enough, but he still had a kink in his neck and a sticky patch of spruce sap on his forearm the fancy shower soap slid right over.

Before wrapping himself in the down duvet on the soft mattress, he crossed the room and stood in front of a framed sketch and photo. The drawing was a depiction of him. The blurb below told the legend of the Toklat Yeti. The photo was of the artist—Helen, with her dark hair gleaming in the sun. She'd never seen him, but he'd seen her from a distance. She'd made the sketch from other people's descriptions and grainy photos taken when Rab hadn't been careful enough.

That hair. Dark and flowing like a river over smooth black rock. And a quick smile that was wide and engaging. She'd searched for him. A lot of people did. But she was different—an unassuming presence during her years working at the lodge. Rab would sometimes see her, out on the tundra with her sketch pad, in the fall before the lodge closed for the season.

He kissed his finger and pressed it to the photo. If only he could touch her for real. Helen had ignited a flame in Rab that no other woman had. And he'd never even talked to her. He tried not to regret that he hadn't revealed himself to her when he had the chance. Years had passed since she'd worked at the lodge, and all he had was this photo and a yearning for someone he would likely never see again.

Not taking his eyes off the photo, Rab retreated to the bed until his furry calves pressed against the foot of it. With arms spread wide, he finally closed his eyes and fell back, bouncing on the mattress but sinking into the cushioning softness of the duvet. With a contented sigh, he wrapped himself up and fell into a sleep that was shorter but deeper than a bear's, snug in its wintery den. His dreams were filled with rippling, obsidian hair and soft curves that were always just out of reach.

HELEN ADJUSTED the mouthpiece to her headset. "It's been eight years since I last worked at Toklat Lodge," she said to the pilot before turning back to the expanse of snowy white beneath the plane.

A forty-something Alaskan, lodge owner, and bush pilot who never seemed to age, Dale wore old-school wool button-ups rather than modern fleece pullovers. Helen had flown with him many times before leaving Alaska and trusted his skills more than any other pilot she'd flown with. His voice held a hint of static as it came through her headphones. "Shoot. You're making me feel old. Seems like two years at most."

Helen grinned. Like many young Alaskans, she'd spent every summer from age eighteen to twenty-four working in the tourism industry. Her various positions at Toklat Lodge had included cleaning rooms, serving food, groundskeeping, and even concierge services. Regardless of her role, her time at the lodge had been amazing.

Since then, law school, a job, and a fiancé in Portland had kept her away . . . until now. When life came crashing down around her this year, she'd longed for the peaceful, carefree days and slower pace of Toklat Lodge. When Dale, her former employer and old family friend, called asking for a favor, she'd jumped at the chance. The timing seemed too good to be true.

Helen slowly let out a breath to calm her racing heart as she shoved away thoughts of the mess she'd left behind.

"Can't talk you into staying all winter, can I, sunshine?"

"Afraid not. I can only take this one month off work. Besides, don't you have the rest of winter covered by your usual guy? I've never met him, but isn't he from Nepal or somewhere?"

"You mean Rab? His family is originally from Tibet," Dale said, his brow wrinkling with concern. "No, no word from him this year."

"You worried?"

"I usually hear from him by now. He sends me a letter. He's old-fashioned that way."

Helen pictured an older man who preferred stationary and a flowing fountain pen to email—romantic but not very practical. "Maybe it got lost in the mail."

"Could be. But he usually pops up before now."

"Maybe he's tired of long, dark winters and is relaxing on a beach somewhere." Helen recalled the need for sun and heat during the darkest days of the year.

"Doubtful. He lives for winter and loves the snow."

"Like the Toklat Yeti," she joked. The area was well known for occasional sightings in the fall, right before the snow fell and the lodge closed each season. Helen had romanticized the legendary monster, filling sketchbooks with likenesses of him based on other people's descriptions.

Of course, she'd never seen the yeti because he wasn't real. But her twenty-four-year-old self had believed in him.

Dale didn't respond.

"Well, his loss, my gain. I can't tell you how much I'm looking forward to some alone time." She planned to meditate, do yoga, play in the snow, and read. The lodge didn't have cell phone or internet access, so she'd preloaded her e-reader with romance novels and several motivational and empowerment books for women.

Time to turn a new page. Helen would leave Toklat Lodge a better, stronger version of herself. Her ex would regret the day he'd left her with an enormous bill for a wedding that hadn't happen.

Who was she kidding? Regret? Her ex didn't

know the meaning of the word. She'd devoted years of her life to him, supporting him through low-paying, dead-end jobs and a second degree. He'd left her only eight months ago and was already engaged again.

But she needed to leave him and all those negative, regretful, resentful feelings in the past. He wasn't looking back, and Helen didn't want to either. This trip was not about getting over a disingenuous, narcissistic user. It was about rediscovering herself.

The lodge came into view, and the plane descended. In winter, the road leading to the lodge served as a runway. Dale brought the Cessna down, slowing as they glided toward the entrance on the plane's skis.

"If you can get your bags, Helen, I'll haul in the supplies."

Together, they emptied all the plane's cargo, including Helen's two bags and some fresh food for her stay, even though the freezer would be full and the pantry stocked with ample dried goods. Off the maintained road system in Alaska, it was best to be prepared for long stretches where the weather prevented resupply or rescue from the air or ground.

After a quick tour around the building to check the heat and electricity—Toklat Lodge thankfully had electricity year-round—Dale looked to the horizon. "Those low clouds are moving back in. You're in for more snow, sunshine." He looked back at Helen. "You've got the satellite communicator?"

"Got it." In an emergency, Helen could get a message out to Dale.

"Well then, let's turn this bird around."

Helen chuckled as she literally helped Dale drag the tail of the plane around so it could take off, back down the road they'd landed on. She'd missed these quintessential Alaska moments. Within minutes, Dale was airborne. She watched until the buzz of the engine faded, and it became a small dot on the horizon.

Then . . . silence.

With eyes closed, Helen filled her lungs. *Yes. This.* Cold, fresh air, and time to do anything she wanted. When she opened her eyes and turned back to the lodge, her gaze fell on the hot tub. *Oh yeah.* What better way to relax than in nice, bubbling, hot water? She'd had little sleep over the last twenty-four hours, and her bed was calling her. But before she climbed under the down duvet, she wanted a soak.

Helen followed a path Dale must have shoveled through the snow toward the tub. He'd been out a few days earlier to prepare things for her. What were the chances he'd winterized it? When she pulled back the cover and steam hit her face, she murmured, "You're the best, Dale."

She trailed her fingers through the water and frowned as she pulled up a wad of white fur. Helen rubbed it between her fingers. Not as coarse as the moose hair she'd occasionally found stuck to tree bark. Longer than rabbit fur, though the same color as an arctic hare's winter coat. A critter had gone for a swim before Dale placed the cover on the tub.

Helen used a skimmer to remove the rest of the hair. The chemicals would've killed any germs, and a little detritus would not put her off. A meditative soak in the falling snow sounded like the perfect way to start The Month of Helen. And since she had the whole lodge to herself, she tossed her bags into the biggest room, named after the biggest mountain—the Denali Suite. She stripped out of her clothes and returned to the hot tub in nothing but her towel. She hung that on the hook near the tub, climbed the platform steps, and stepped in, enveloping herself in hot, steamy bliss.

CHAPTER TWO

Rab's stomach woke him up. It could have been the gnawing sensation of hunger or the audible growling. One thing he was certain of, voles were not on the dinner menu. Nope. Tonight he'd eat human food.

He tossed back the duvet and stretched as he glanced down his furry body. He'd gone all summer sans clothing. A yeti in the wilds during an Alaska summer didn't need quick-dry fabric when their fur naturally repelled water. But human activities like cooking and lodge repairs often called for protective coverings, so Rab stored some clothes at the lodge.

His stomach rumbled again. First things first.

Dale always made sure the pantry was well

stocked, and he knew Rab's weakness for olives. Canned black olives were better than grubs any day, but jumbo greens with their pimento jelly centers, or less firm but more interesting kalamatas, were so much better.

Yeti didn't prance, but Rab came close on his way down the stairs to the kitchen, mouth watering in anticipation.

The pantry didn't disappoint. He opened a jar of manzanillas and, since he hadn't filed his claws yet, slid olives onto each—yeti claws were nature's cocktail toothpick. He sported olives three deep on the claw of each pointer finger when he heard a noise.

Rab stilled, spotting two unfamiliar food totes against the kitchen wall. He'd walked right by them, too focused on filling his stomach to notice.

When Rab arrived earlier in the day, he could tell Dale had recently been at the lodge, but hadn't left his customary note. Was it because he'd been planning another supply trip today?

Maybe Rab *had* heard a plane earlier?

Olive jar in hand, he went out a side door and around to the front of the lodge. New snow was filling in recent tracks from a takeoff and landing. Rab narrowed his gaze as he took in two sets of footprints.

Yeti generally avoided human contact, not wanting to end up in a test lab, zoo, or stuffed in a museum. Safety first. Of course, Dale knew this. He wouldn't have brought anyone to the lodge that Rab didn't know.

He followed a set of footprints around the other side of the building, and his hair lifted across his shoulders and back when he smelled it. Chlorine.

Steam rose from the hot tub. The hot tub he was certain he'd covered.

Rab could blame any number of things for his dull reflexes. But when the woman in the hot tub looked up and saw Rab, he stood motionless, in full sight, in the middle of the deck. Like a bull moose on the bare tundra during hunting season—exposed and unmissable.

Before he could stop himself, he blurted, "Helen?"

She screamed.

HELEN SHRIEKED. Any naked woman would if she thought she was alone and opened her eyes to find someone standing in front of her. Her feet slipped against the bed of the hot tub, unable to find purchase as she tried to boost herself up and out, to flee.

She caught her balance and stopped windmilling her arms as it sank in that this person knew her name.

While trying to cover her goodies with both arms, she scanned his white furry head and body, covering broad shoulders, muscular chest, and solid legs. People in Alaska often wore outfits trimmed in fur, but this guy sported white, fluffy fur from head to toe.

Helen froze to the spot, completely dumbfounded. *He isn't wearing fur. It's part of him.* She made a slow blink. *It can't be anything else.* The Toklat Yeti stood before her.

"You're real?" she managed to squeak. Was she dreaming? Hallucinating? Had she stayed in the hot tub too long?

He looked like the descriptions, but no one had ever mentioned he could talk. And he knew her name, which made Helen's heart race like she'd spiked her coffee with espresso. *Shouldn't I be scared? Freaking out?* Instead, nervous excitement bubbled up inside.

"Sorry, sorry. I didn't mean to frighten you. I

didn't know anyone else was here." The yeti's deep voice sent a shiver—more like a thrill—through her body. He held up a furry hand, shielding his eyes. "And I didn't see your tits—um, breasts. I . . . Oh man, uh . . . Want a towel?"

Helen plopped back into the water, submerging herself. Her nipples had pebbled from the cold—or from the deep rumbling of his voice—but they puckered even more knowing he'd noticed.

What was wrong with her? It had been way too long since her body had gotten any kind of attention. "I have a towel," Helen said, trying to make her voice sound strong. "If you'll just turn around, I'll get it."

"Oh, right. Yeah, sorry. Should have thought of that." The furry, seven-foot frame pivoted, as agile and graceful as a quarterback but bigger than a linebacker. But *his* bulk wasn't padding.

Helen stepped out of the tub. Her hands shook while she slipped into her boots and wrapped herself in the oversized towel. "Okay, I'm decent."

The creature slowly turned, his hand covering his eyes, but fingers splayed as he peeked through them. He dropped his arm as he took in her covered figure and let out a breath. "Man, sorry about that. I didn't know Dale was planning another trip here so soon. And no offense, but I don't know why he left you out here. He's usually more careful around me and all. He—"

Helen held up a hand, and the yeti stopped his rush of words. *Is he nervous?* How could he be? He was a giant, fur-covered being who'd have no trouble walking away from the lodge in the middle of this snowstorm. Helen, on the other hand, was a wet, naked woman who would soon lose the warmth from the hot tub and freeze to death if she didn't get back inside.

But before she locked herself in a building in the middle of nowhere—with the freaking Toklat Yeti on the porch—she needed some answers from the muscular monster. "How do you know my name?"

The yeti's cheeks lifted, and the corners of his eyes creased with a warm smile. His face was the same deep azure blue as the palms of his hands, complimenting eyes the color of thin sheets of glacial ice. "You used to sketch pictures of me."

Helen's heart fluttered at his admission. She recalled brisk autumn afternoons when she would strike out from the lodge with her bear spray and sketch pad, hoping to glimpse the yeti. With her whole life before her, anything had seemed possible.

And the mystique of the furry man-beast had always intrigued her. Truly, she'd had a yeti crush.

"There's a whole thing about us on the wall in the Foraker Suite," Rab explained.

In all her imaginings, she hadn't pictured how masculine and powerful he'd be. *Oh god.* She was checking him out again.

He must have noticed because he moved a hand as if to cover himself—not that anything showed under all the fur. "I, uh, usually wear clothes around humans."

He'd pass for a sexy, bearded man with white hair—and blue skin—if he'd been wearing jeans and a shirt. She tried not to look at the juncture of his furry legs. "You're really *the* Toklat Yeti?"

"The one and only . . . I mean, there are other yeti, but none like me." He stood a little straighter.

Helen arched an eyebrow. "What does that mean?"

"Means I like to romp around naked in the mountains all summer. But come winter, I appreciate Egyptian cotton sheets and cooked meat."

"And olives?" She motioned to the jar in his hand and the little green things on his claws, her lips twitching.

The yeti looked down as if he'd forgotten he held

anything. He sighed and rolled his eyes. "Yeah, I like olives. I also thought I was alone, okay?" He shook his free hand as if trying to dislodge the brined orbs from his long, pointy claws. It didn't work. He turned away from her, apparently sucking them off his fingers before turning back. He scowled. "Don't laugh at me."

Helen bit back a smile. "Definitely not laughing." She was not about to make fun of this giant guy. But her head spun. She'd finally seen the Toklat Yeti. And he wasn't some bipedal, bear-like creature. He could talk, knew her name, and liked olives. Also, he was kind of hot—in a big, furry, adorable way.

She pulled her towel more tightly around herself as the heat from her soak faded. "So, how do you know what's in the Foraker Suite and, uh, what are you doing here?"

He lifted his chin, and his voice deepened as he declared, "I'm the Toklat Lodge winter caretaker. The Foraker Suite is *my* room from October through April each year."

Helen stilled. He couldn't be the winter caretaker. That was her job, at least until the regular guy showed up. She was supposed to spend a quiet month in the wilderness by herself, meditating and getting her life back on track. "I'm the winter caretaker, at least for the next few weeks. Dale just dropped me off."

"What?"

"Plus, he *has* a longtime caretaker. Guy named Rab who . . . writes . . . letters." Helen closed her eyes and nodded as she put the pieces together. The *yeti*, not an older letter-writing gentleman, watched the lodge each winter. *"You're* Rab."

"Rabten. My friends call me Rab."

Friends like Dale. She was going to kill that pilot. "Well, Rab, Dale didn't get your letter this year, so he hired me and said the lodge was mine for a month." And she really wanted—no, needed—this month alone. "So, you're off the hook for a few weeks. You could go . . ." *Where?* His choices were limited. "A month in Hawaii isn't your style, is it?"

He crossed his arms. "Not so much. And I've been sleeping on the hard ground for months. I'm not giving up my bed."

A gust of wind caught the edge of Helen's towel, exposing a little more leg than she would have liked and sending a snowy breeze up her body. She shivered. *If I turn him out of the lodge tonight, I'll be the monster.*

"Why don't you go in," Rab offered. "I could stand here for hours, but you're cold. I'll close the hot tub, and you can, uh . . ." As his eyes skated over her towel-clad body, Helen shivered for a different reason. "Go shower and dress. We can talk after."

Helen considered arguing, but her teeth were chattering. She nodded and went into the lodge. Apparently the muscular monster, better known as the Toklat Yeti, would be Helen's new roomie.

RAB WATCHED Helen retreat into the lodge, his heart thumping and a heat in his groin he hadn't experienced in years.

Helen. The elusive beauty with a sketch pad. All those years ago, if he'd let her see him, would she have smiled and waved?

Rab groaned. She *had* finally seen him, and her first reaction had been to scream. He rested his hands on the edge of the hot tub and let his head hang, recalling her lush, curvy body and the tits he wanted to cup in his calloused palms.

Damn that Dale. And damn the postal service. Rab *had* written a letter. And even if he hadn't, why would Dale think he wouldn't show after all these years?

Now he was stuck here with a raven-haired beauty who had been counting on a month alone.

He pulled the cover over the hot tub. Well, she'd better be hungry because it was Rab's first night in the lodge, and he intended to feast. Hopefully, Helen was up for a celebration.

CHAPTER THREE

Helen strode to her bedroom. Tension and stress were supposed to be melting away now that she was at the Toklat Lodge, damnit. But she had her shoulders shrugged up to her ears, her fists clenched in her towel, and her teeth grinding, which she had to stop before she gave herself a headache.

She was wound so tight. But was it any wonder? In the last couple of days, she'd moved out of her apartment, put her stuff in storage, and donated all the shit her ex had left behind when he'd dumped her. She'd put in a full day of work at the law firm before catching a red-eye from Portland through Seattle to Fairbanks. For her final leg of travel, she'd transferred to Dale's bush plane to get here.

Would the hot tub have relaxed her if a furry monster hadn't interrupted her soak? Hard to say.

The yeti was real, not the daydream of a jet-lagged, sleep-deprived woman. The seven-foot man-beast covered in fur had seen her naked. And she might have liked it.

Helen toweled off, skin tingling as she remembered how he'd looked at her. It'd clearly been too long since she'd been with anyone. Being overtired, her hormones were out of whack. Nothing more.

Once she'd dried her hair and dressed in a cozy sweater and leggings, she picked up the satellite communicator. Should she message Dale to pick her up? Since his real caretaker had arrived, he didn't need her.

Plus, the whole idea of a month in the wilderness might be extreme. The law firm wasn't happy with her taking time off. Her friends and colleagues viewed her trip like an adventure comparable to reaching the North Pole on skis.

Her mother's reaction had been mixed. She'd been surprised at Helen's decision but hadn't discouraged her. Although born and raised in rural Alaska, her mother had lived in the Portland area since Helen had graduated high school. She was now so urbanized that she'd sent Helen off with a global positioning system tracker. At this moment, Mom could be watching a flashing dot on a map on her computer screen.

She rubbed her thumb over the communicator's power switch but didn't turn it on. What would she do if she went home now? She didn't have a new apartment yet and would be forced to couch surf. Her family, friends, and the law firm would be happier if she returned early. But would she?

As she turned the device over in her hands, food scents permeated her room—sautéed onions, garlic, and the earthy smell of mushrooms. Helen inhaled deeply, and a hint of flame-cooked meat hit her nose. Rab must've started the grill and, by the smell of it, the yeti could cook.

Curiosity and hunger won out. She dropped the communicator on her bed and marched downstairs, determined to ignore the awkwardness of facing a person who'd just seen her naked. Although, technically, Rab had been naked too. He just had a lot more hair covering his pleasurable parts.

Helen snorted. *Pleasurable parts? Where did that come from?* Private *parts.*

She would not let her mind wander and imagine what those might look like on a yeti. No, not going there.

The aroma became stronger as Helen neared the kitchen, and her mouth started to water. She saw Rab at the grill next to the hot tub. Though barefoot, he wore jeans, a T-shirt, and an apron with the words *Go Kiss a Moose*. The cartoon moose printed on the front had big, red lips. The whole getup should have looked ridiculous. And yet he pulled it off, oozing confidence and masculinity.

Clearly, Helen was too hungry and tired to think straight.

She pushed into her boots and shuffled outside to talk to him. "Hi," she said, her heart beating wildly, which had to be nerves. Rab towered over her by a solid foot and a half.

Helen cleared her throat and said, "Can we start over? Now that I'm . . ." *not naked*. "Well, anyway. I'm Helen." She stuck out her hand. "It's nice to meet you, finally." So much for not sounding flustered.

That's when she realized Rab wore big oven mitts on each hand—moose heads with floppy antlers that covered his forearms and red cartoon lips that formed a mouth between the thumb and fingers.

He lifted a hand. "I gotta watch the fur around the flame. Let me just get these steaks."

"Oh, right, yeah, of course." All that fur around the grill would be dangerous.

With a set of long grill tongs, he turned over several steaks, a couple of chicken breasts, and a halibut fillet, releasing a smell any omnivore would appreciate. How much did a yeti eat? Then he set down the tongs, pulled off a mitt, and offered Helen a big furry hand. "Rabten. Call me Rab. It's nice to meet *you*."

Rab's hand closed around hers like a much-loved baseball mitt—soft and supple but with separate fingers. While fur covered the back of his hand, his fingers and palm were a smooth, beryl blue. And his claws were pointed, black, and olive-free. It looked like he took care not to bend his fingers to keep from scratching her. His palm felt like suede against her skin. The tickle of his fur reminded her of downy-soft rabbit pelts. As a child, her mother had sewn them as trim around her parka.

"Um," he said, glancing down at their hands with a smile and a raised brow. "I need to get the fish."

A warm flush crept over her, chasing away the chill from being out in the snow again. Helen dropped Rab's hand and took a step back for good measure. She'd not only been staring at his hand but holding it with both of hers. "Sorry," she squeaked.

In no culture she was familiar with was it okay to inspect someone's hand after an introduction.

"Like daggers, right?"

Rab's question pulled Helen out of her visual cataloging of the yeti's features. She stared at him blankly. "I'm sorry?"

"My claws," he clarified before removing the halibut and moving meat and vegetables around the grill. He motioned to his hands, once again covered with oven mitts. "They're like daggers. Perfect for gutting rodents, but . . ."

Rab tapered off and gave her a side-eye. "I probably shouldn't have mentioned gutting."

Helen realized her mouth hung open. She closed it with a gulp. *His hands are deadly weapons.* She cleared her throat. *No, they're* tools *used for hunting.* "It's fine. I mean, I rarely think about gutting animals. When I buy chicken, someone has already done it for me." *With a knife, not their claws.*

"Right. Never been inside a grocery store myself, but I've seen the packaging." He shifted the rest of the meat and vegetables to the serving platter. "Anyway, I need to trim my claws. They're impractical when I'm at the lodge. I won't be hunting for my dinner or defending myself from an ornery grizzly bear for the next six months."

"You look bigger than a griz." she mumbled before realizing she might as well have squeezed one of Rab's biceps, batted her eyelashes, and said, "A big guy like you could take a griz any day."

Shit.

Rab puffed up a bit, his shirt and apron stretching tight across his impressive pecs. "I don't mean to brag, but . . . Ursus versus yeti? I'd crush the bear every time." Utterly confident, his eyes focused steadily on her. If she'd received a look like that in a bar, she'd have rolled her eyes and walked away. But coming from Rab, she blushed and stayed put.

Helen's lips stretched in a grin. Not the forced *stop worrying about me, even though my fiancé left me, I'm fine* smile she'd adopted recently. This one was real.

He turned off the grill. "You hungry?"

He'd cooked enough food for six people, or perhaps exactly the right amount for one hungry yeti and herself. She inhaled the delicious smells coming from the platter, her empty stomach rumbling with pleasure. "I'm starving."

"Excellent." Rab hefted the serving platter and preceded her inside. "Because tonight we celebrate and feast."

The message to Dale could wait until tomorrow.

He wouldn't fly out tonight in the dark and the snow anyway.

Besides, Helen wanted to celebrate—to feast with the yeti.

"Hell, yeah," she said. "You want a martini? I know we have olives . . . unless you ate them all."

RAB AND HELEN pulled one of the lodge's couches closer to the central fireplace in the great room. Their bellies were full, the wine bottle was empty, and the fire crackled, toasty warm.

Rab plopped down on one end of the couch. He crossed and rested his travel-weary legs on the small coffee table and rotated his ankles to stretch his sore muscles. An overwhelming sense of peace and security washed over him at being well fed and in a climate-controlled shelter with four walls and plumbing.

Returning to the lodge was always a season change, both literally and figuratively. Each year Rab celebrated, sometimes with Dale but more often by himself, and never with such good company. Sharing the night with Helen this year was like entering a new and better era. One in which he wasn't alone.

Helen kicked off her shoes and pulled her legs under her at the other end of the couch. "I haven't eaten that much since . . . well, ever. This tops any holiday feast I've ever had. Everything was delicious. Especially the thing you did with the scallops."

"Bacon-wrapped scallops?"

"Genius." She groaned with pleasure. Her head thudded against the back of the couch, and the remaining wine in her glass nearly sloshed out. Rab slipped the stemware out of her hand and set it on the side table.

Helen nestled into the corner, facing him with her legs bent and her feet on the cushion next to his thigh. "Where did a cook like you learn how to yeti?"

"If you meant, where did a yeti like me learn how to cook—"

Her brow furrowed. "That's what I said."

He couldn't stop a grin, tipsy Helen was adorable. "Of course. Must be the wine affecting my hearing."

"A side effect of a good cab," she said with the dignified authority only a martini and several glasses of wine could provide. "So, how did you go from disemboweling rodents to cooking a five-star meal?"

"When the crowds thin in the fall, I help here in the kitchen." He drained his glass and set it on the table next to Helen's. "How do you think I managed to score such great cuts of meat and seafood?" He cleared his throat. "The chef and I have an arrangement."

Helen's brows shot up. "Oh? Sounds intriguing. Don't tell me you're the source of the smoked salmon?"

Rab laced his fingers behind his head and uncrossed his legs as they were threatening to cramp. "Reindeer. I keep predators away from a couple of farms out in Delta. I get meat in return. The meat goes to the lodge and—"

"No way," Helen interrupted as she leaned forward in apparent excitement. "The reindeer sausage?"

He smiled at her enthusiasm. "That's part of it. And the chef leaves me things in the freezer. Anything with an R on it is mine."

"So, you're to thank for my favorite sausage gravy and biscuits."

"I'm just the delivery guy."

Helen snorted and wiggled her toes under his leg. She didn't even seem to notice she'd done it, but for Rab, physical contact was rare and, therefore, precious. His heart thudded in his chest with such force he was afraid it shook the couch.

While he tried to calm his circulatory system, Helen circled back to their conversation over dinner. "So, Rabten, the Toklat Yeti . . . You wander the Alaska Range in summer, stay at the lodge in winter, never miss the Halloween bash in Denali, and host a New Year's Eve party here at the lodge for your friends . . .?"

She paused. "Wait. Are your friends yeti? Are there other yeti? I mean you had to have parents." She forced a laugh, then her eyes narrowed. "Right?"

"I have a yeti mother and father. They were semi-nomadic, but they're getting older now and live in a remote cabin," he explained. "And yes, I have yeti friends." He chuckled as her eyes grew wide. "I have a few human friends too, but Tseten and my coworkers from Mountain High Guiding Service—Pema, Denzin, and Dorje—are all yeti. Dorje's had a rough year and probably won't come to the parties this winter."

"But your other friends will be at this Halloween party you keep mentioning?"

"They live closer to Anchorage but usually make it." Halloween was the one time a year yeti could be social with humans they didn't know. "Dale picks me up and flies me to Denali to party. If you don't mind, I'll use your satellite thingy to send him a message, remind him." Before he lost his nerve he blurted, "You should come."

"To a Halloween party?" Helen shook her head. "I don't have a costume."

"We'll find you one." Rab grinned, imagining Helen in one of those sexy costumes—kitten, nurse, barmaid—didn't matter. Except he didn't want anyone else staring at her cleavage—those gorgeous breasts. "Maybe we could bring a sheet. You could go as a ghost."

Her eyebrow slowly rose. "A sheet?" She didn't sound onboard with the idea. "So you go to your Halloween thing in Denali and host a New Year's Eve party here—which would be amazing. This place would be gorgeous all decked out in lights and spruce greens."

The parties were a good time, and now he wanted Helen to be at the next one. Impossible though, since she'd only be in Alaska for a month.

She continued. "And you guide climbers in Denali National Park in the spring. How does that work? People must realize you're . . ." She leaned toward him, gesturing with her hand as her eyes roamed his body.

"Covered in fur?"

She slowly cocked her head. "Well, yeah. And *blue*."

"Halloween is easy. I was born in my costume. I've got this fake bandolier, so I go as an albino Wookiee. I wait to arrive till the beer has been flowing for a while. No one knows what I am—well, except the few who do know. It's the best."

"Okay, and what about while you're climbing Denali?"

"I'm covered in bright nylon and usually wear ski goggles and a face mask. The clients don't know. I put zinc oxide on any exposed skin. It covers the blue and protects against the elements. I'm just the prematurely white-haired, quiet dude with larger-than-normal canines and a lot of white facial hair."

She leaned back and crossed her arms, a skeptical look on her face. "And the clients really can't tell?"

"I know how to be inconspicuous. If you're too friendly, people ask questions, want to know who you are, and try to look you up after the climb. If you don't say much and fade into the background, no one remembers you."

A few seconds ticked by as Helen regarded him, her gaze softening. "That's sad, Rab. Heartbreaking."

His heart thundered again, and he forced a

nonchalant shrug, shifting his achy legs. He stretched the right one by pointing and flexing his foot. Had he hiked twenty miles that morning or thirty? "You get used to it."

Sorta. More like he'd made his peace.

He wanted to change the subject. Helen glowed, was full of life and able to live it any way she chose. She had to have a better story. "What about you? What brings you to the Toklat Lodge at the start of winter?"

Rab expected her eyes to sparkle. For her to tell him she was between adventures. Maybe she'd quit a job and was getting ready for a stint in the Peace Corps. Anything seemed possible for the girl with the sketch pad and gleam in her eye. She only had to reach for it.

But Helen's face fell. And instead of the gleam he expected, her eyes welled with tears. "I came here to remember who I am. It's supposed to be The Month of Helen." She made air quotes. "I loved my time here when I was younger. I hoped that by returning I could step back from what my life has become—who I've become—and rediscover myself. I thought I knew. But life has a way of channeling you down paths. Past goals fade. Other goals form, but they're no longer your own. Your goals are his goals, and it's all out of your control. And then he leaves you. And you have nothing. And . . ." Helen clapped a hand over her mouth and pulled her knees to her chest. "Sorry."

Rab hated whoever *he* was. Stupid son of a mangy fox. "Don't apologize," he said, scooting over and sliding an arm around her shoulders.

People who raved about bear hugs never had a yeti hug. He pulled her to his side, and she melted into him like she was overdue for caring arms to hold her. Rab could relate. You became acutely aware of what you were missing when you went without for too long.

"I'll help you celebrate The Month of Helen," he said.

Tears streaked down her cheeks, and her arms and scent—fresh, like the early morning tundra covered in dew—wrapped around him. Rab patted her head and ran a hand down her thick, dark hair, hating the asshole who'd hurt her, but also grateful because it had driven her into his arms.

No. He really shouldn't think that way.

Unfortunately, at this tender moment when Helen needed him, his leg muscle seized. He sprang up from the couch stumbling around trying to loosen the knot. He growled obscenities under his breath as Helen looked on with wide eyes.

"What is it?" she asked.

"Leg cramp," he bit out between gritted teeth. "Will pass." He slid the offending leg out to the side and leaned the other way in a stretch as he let out a hiss.

She jumped to her feet. "Wait here." As if he could go anywhere. "I have a muscle roller."

"W-what?"

But Helen had flown up the stairs. She returned moments later, triumphantly waving what looked like a blue rolling pin. "This will help."

"I'm not making cookies here," he ground out as he widened his stance.

Helen chuckled. "It's for rolling out muscles, not dough." She looked from him to the contraption in her hands. "It will help ease your cramp. Let me show you."

Rab's gaze slid to hers and then away. "It's my inner thigh," he said by way of warning. She did not need to get anywhere near his groin with her hands or the muscle roller.

She wasn't deterred. No, she crawled between his legs, placed the foam stick against the seizing muscle, and slowly rolled it up and down. She worked his muscle like it was a lump of cold, stiff dough.

Surprisingly, it helped. Bit by bit, the knot eased. "Oh," he growled, "that's good."

As if encouraged, Helen expanded her range, running the tool from his knee up to uh . . .

Maybe it felt a little too good. He pulled away before he embarrassed himself. If he became any more aroused, his dick would drop from its protective sheath. And no matter how well hidden by fur or secured behind his jeans, he wouldn't be able to hide his raging yeti erection.

He turned away and shook out his leg. "That did the trick. Thank you."

She got to her feet and twirled the roller. "Yeah, these are great. Need anything else rubbed?"

Rab blinked at the loaded question.

An adorable pink, which had nothing to do with the hot fire, colored her cheeks. "I didn't mean . . ."

He cleared his throat. "So anyway, I was about to say, I won't ruin your Month of Helen at the lodge. Don't change your plans. I'll stay out of your way." *Don't leave me.*

Big, glassy eyes looked up at him. "I'll stay." She took his hand in hers. "But please don't hide or fade into the background. I want you to be yourself while I'm here."

His heart swelled. Though he wanted to scoop her back into his arms, he gave her hand a light squeeze instead. "Deal."

CHAPTER FOUR

A delicious warmth enveloped Helen as she slowly woke. She was at the lodge, basically on vacation. If she wanted, she could sleep all day. And other than the slight pounding in the back of her head, a sore hip, and a fuzzy mouth, she felt great. She'd had too much wine. Too much food. But such a fun time. Like, the best. It had been years since she'd woken up with an afterglow from a great evening.

All thanks to Rab. The yeti. He made her smile. Made her feel special. Made her feel . . . tingly in her girly bits. Her body flushed as she gradually became aware of her surroundings.

Yeah, she felt warm and cozy. But it wasn't a weighted blanket across her upper body. It was a furry arm. And the warmth against her back? A solid chest and a beating yeti heart. Her hip hurt because it was pressing into the seam of the couch cushion. She remained still, resisting the urge to bolt upright, even as her heart took off at a gallop.

They'd talked into the wee hours of the morning and fallen asleep in front of the fire—on opposite ends of the couch. Helen had a vague memory of waking up chilled and crawling across the cushions into Rab's waiting arms. His clean scent, like a warm chinook wind, had surrounded her as she snuggled into him. He was like a giant teddy bear, though she'd bet that he'd hate anyone comparing him to a bear or a soft plush toy.

But his fur was like silk. It would feel so good against her naked . . . Nope. Not going to think about skin on fur contact. Except she already had and a pulse of heat throbbed between her legs.

Rab was a muscular wall behind her. He made her feel protected, and not just physically. After spending the night talking with him, Helen had the impression he would stand by the people he cared about. He'd never leave them high and dry because he was "bored", unlike her ex.

She listened to Rab's steady, even breaths, then cracked open one eyelid. The large windows beyond the central fireplace looked out on the Alaska Range. Dark mountain peaks silhouetted against a faint yellow glow on the horizon, the promise of a sunrise —around ten a.m. this time of year—still hours away.

The sky was clear. Dale could fly today. She could message him, ask for a pickup, abandon her plans for the month, and do what her family and friends considered best.

No. Helen wanted to stay, and Rab wanted her to stay too. The corners of her mouth turned up. She closed her eye and pulled Rab's arm more tightly around her. His fingers twitched in his sleep, a claw grazing her boob. She ignored the spark of sensation. They were becoming friends—friends who snuggled on the couch, evidently, but still friends. Plus, he was a yeti.

But as she drifted back to sleep, her core still throbbing, she wondered, *what if . . .*

RAB STARED down at the sleeping woman in his arms. *Fuck.* He never wanted to let go. And yet, if he didn't, Helen would know exactly where his mind was. Maybe he could convince her that all yeti woke up with morning wood. Just laugh—or cringe

—it off? He'd been fighting it since he'd drifted awake.

One thing was certain. Rab would trade a night in a bed for a night with Helen anywhere. Cuddling with her had been cozier than a wolf den full of pups —and a hell of a lot sexier.

He couldn't remember a more amazing night. His kind were few and far between, and connecting with others wasn't easy. Plus he lived a transient lifestyle, and Alaska was a big place. So he appreciated the few times a year when he was around people. Halloween, when he could be himself but also be the guy with the best costume in the room. The climbing season—but that was intense. And late fall at the lodge, when they were down to a skeleton crew. This year, he'd missed the closing of the lodge. He'd wandered farther east than he'd intended, and early-season storms had delayed him.

Helen stirred, her ass nestling against him in the most tantalizing way, and she hugged his palm against her chest. Her tits were millimeters from his fingers, and he was trying hard not to cop a feel. He didn't want his claws marring her perfect breasts.

He needed to do something before his erection became big, bold, and all too obvious. But as Rab attempted to distract himself from her soft, curvy body pressed against his, Helen twitched in her sleep, almost rolling off the couch.

Rab instinctively gripped her to him, but she yelped, "Ouch, your claws!"

"Oh, shit." Rab let her go, nearly tipping the couch as he launched his body over the back to get out of the way. "Are you hurt?"

Helen sat up and pulled off her sweater to look down at her chest. "Just startled, that's all." But red bloomed through her T-shirt.

"Shit, Helen. You're bleeding."

"I'm sure it's nothing, I—"

He cut her off as he scooped her up, careful to keep his claws well away from her clothes and body. "There's a first aid kit in my bathroom."

He was vaguely aware she'd looped her arms around his neck as he rushed her up the stairs.

"Rab, I'm sure it's fine."

What if she wasn't okay? What if he'd really hurt her? What if he'd scarred her? He gently set her on the bathroom counter. His hands were at the hem of her shirt. "May I?" he asked, and she helped him lift it off.

Despite his concern, his horny gaze zeroed in on her tits. Did he imagine it, or did she arch her back, lifting her chest in encouragement? The color of her sheer bra reminded him of the deep blue sky before a winter moonrise. The blush of a nipple beneath the taut fabric teased him, and a full breast filled each cup. He wanted to touch them. Pull down her bra and circle her nipples with his fingers. His tongue.

"Look," she said, pulling his focus away from her boobs. "It's only a scratch."

He disagreed with her assessment. Blood seeped from two parallel cuts across her chest, right over her heart. A drop of red trickled before he caught it with her balled-up T-shirt. "Those should be cleaned, bandaged."

Helen moved to take the shirt from him. "Rab, I'm fine."

He pressed the shirt against the wounds. "Keep pressure on it." He waited till she held the shirt against herself, then turned on the hot water and picked up the bar of soap.

"Yes, sir," she responded as he recited the alphabet under his breath, ensuring he scrubbed his furry hands long enough to remove all bacteria. "I'll sit here on your bathroom counter in my bra and apply pressure to a couple of light scratches if it makes you feel better."

He slowed, glancing at her as he rinsed his hands.

She had a hint of a smile on her lips. "Rab, you didn't mean to scratch me, and they're not deep."

He swallowed. "No, I didn't mean to, but it might have been worse. I intended to cut and file my claws today. It's a lengthy process. The claws on one hand get in the way while I trim the claws on the other hand. I should have done it yesterday."

Helen reached out and gripped his forearm. She probably meant it to be soothing, but it only quickened his heartbeat. "I can help you."

His mouth opened and closed before he finally said, "You'd do that?"

Her brows arched in surprise. "Of course."

It seemed more intimate than accidentally seeing someone naked in the hot tub. But he supposed to her it was only a manicure—though a heavy-duty one —like at a nail salon.

Rab nodded. "Okay, yeah. Thanks. That would be good."

She dropped the shirt in the sink. The bleeding had slowed. The red welts didn't look too bad. Which meant Rab's eyes wandered, this time to the simple chain she wore. A small, pale-blue, enamel snowflake rested just below the hollow of her throat. He wanted to lean down and kiss that hollow and those breasts he ached to palm.

As if responding to his thoughts, her nipples puckered.

Shit. What was he doing? He snapped his attention back to the cuts. "Let's get some antibacterial cream on these," he said before daring to raise his sheepish gaze to her face once more.

Helen looked amused, as if she knew what he'd really been looking at. "I can manage." She slid off the counter. "Then it's time for coffee."

A wave of disappointment washed over him. He'd been eager to care for her. "I'll start a pot."

"How do you feel about me reading while I drink my coffee?" Her tone was cautious but defiant, like she thought he might not approve.

But he imagined himself seated across from her, companionable silence between them as they both lost themselves in a good story. "Only if I can too." He grinned, thinking of the stack of books and magazines he looked forward to reading over winter.

She rewarded him with a wide smile. "Perfect. After, we'll trim your claws."

Rab's heart thudded. It did sound perfect.

CHAPTER FIVE

Helen stared at herself in the Denali Suite's bathroom mirror. Two parallel, red slashes ran across her chest, ending at her left bra cup.

She'd been marked by the yeti. The corner of her mouth rose.

Why did that make her smile, and why did she secretly hope his claw scrapes would leave a scar?

Because she never wanted to forget her night with Rab and waking up in his arms. Even if it had all been innocent.

Mostly.

She'd shamelessly drawn Rab's attention to her breasts while he fussed over the cuts. But when her nipples had gone hard under the lustful look in his eye, she'd backpedaled. Because what the hell did she think she was doing? Rab was a fellow lodge caretaker, a friend now, and a yeti. A hot yeti . . . But still.

Since arriving at Toklat Lodge—less than twenty-four hours ago, she'd felt happier than she had in years. Being alone at the lodge would have been relaxing, but she wouldn't have been wearing a permanent grin too.

All the more reason to get these lusty impulses in check. No more flirting with Rab. She refused to risk his friendship.

She removed her bra, leaned toward the mirror to see the cuts better, and smeared them with antibacterial cream.

They were awkward to bandage, but she managed to cover them with gauze held in place with medical tape. Instead of putting a bra on over the bulky bandage, she pulled on a camisole, followed by yoga pants and a baggy sweatshirt. She grabbed her e-reader and the toiletry bag with her nail clippers and emery boards—even if they were unlikely to make a dent on Rab's rigid claws—and padded downstairs.

She smelled coffee halfway to the kitchen.

Though always an alluring scent, this was a fancy café espresso level of good, and the lodge didn't have an espresso machine.

The table they'd used last night now held an insulated pot of coffee and one mug—along with cloth napkins and silverware. The yeti had set the table. The celebratory dinner had been outstanding, but this was just . . . breakfast.

Rab emerged from the kitchen carrying a teapot and a bone china teacup. His step faltered when he saw her, his focus drifting to her chest. "Did the bleeding stop?"

Her stomach did a backflip under his blue gaze, remembering what it had done to her nipples earlier. "Yes," She managed, the room suddenly feeling hot.

"Good," he rumbled, his gaze flitting back to her covered wound before gesturing to the table. "I hope you like oatmeal. I started it last night. It's reheating on the stove. Have a seat."

She watched him set the teapot, cup, and saucer next to his place setting before disappearing back into the kitchen.

For someone who spent half the year outdoors, Rab was so . . . domestic, which she frankly found charming. But oatmeal? Not the same level as bacon-wrapped scallops.

"I'm okay with just coffee," Helen called as Rab returned from the kitchen carrying two bowls.

"It's the middle of winter in the mountains. You need more than coffee. And you're still standing. Sit." He placed a bowl at each of their settings before pulling Helen's chair back for her.

She unfroze and sat as he pushed in her chair. "Thanks, Rab. I . . ." she trailed off, still absorbing the scene before her and not sure what to say.

"Do you take cream?" He grimaced. "It's boxed, of course. Not as good as fresh, but it tastes better than muskrat. Take my word for it."

She would. "No, thanks. I take my coffee black."

But he was already on his way back to the kitchen. "We'll need it for the oatmeal."

As she reached for the coffee pot, she eyed the bowl in front of her. If oatmeal was in there somewhere, she couldn't see it. A rainbow of wild, Alaska berries—thawed from the freezer—made a striking mix of reds, blues, and blacks. Rab had drizzled ribbons of golden honey across the fruit and garnished it with sliced, roasted almonds. A work of art.

Rab placed a small pitcher on the table and sat down. Though his claws were still clearly in the way, he picked up the teapot with one hand, held the lid with the other, and poured himself a cup of tea. Like he was getting ready to entertain the queen. Then he poured a thin stream of cream on his oatmeal. He looked to Helen, an eyebrow raised in question. "Oatmeal's better with cream," he said, "even if it's shelf stable."

Helen had her coffee mug cradled in both hands as she watched him. She nodded and he poured a small moat of white around the berries in her bowl.

Rab sipped at his tea, then ate a spoonful of oatmeal. He let out a contented sigh. A moment later, he looked to Helen. "Don't you like oatmeal? Did I burn the coffee?" His eyes dipped to her chest. "Do the cuts hurt?"

She shook her head, realizing that she'd been sitting there staring at him. "No, they don't hurt. I'm fine. And the coffee is exceptionally good." She took another sip and hummed with appreciation.

But oatmeal? It was so thick and stodgy. Plus, Helen rarely ate breakfast. Several cups of black coffee got her through to lunch.

He made it for me. I have to at least try it. She set down the mug and picked up her spoon, scooping a small sample of the yeti's porridge into her mouth. Immediately, warm spice hit her nose. "Mmm . . . nutmeg."

Rab sipped his tea and nodded.

Spice was only the beginning. Cream and honey accentuated the berries, which not only popped with color but flavor as well. The combination with the plump, steel-cut oats and crunch of roasted nuts made this worthy of a brunch in Gourmet magazine. Not stodgy in the least.

The gluey muck from the instant packets had nothing on this. It satisfied like a bowl of biscuits with reindeer sausage gravy. Okay, that might be taking it too far. But it was excellent and more heart-healthy.

"So good," Helen managed to mumble between spoonfuls.

Rab, who'd already ate his portion, leaned back and crossed his legs. He sipped his tea and watched as she all but licked the bowl. "Glad you like it," he said before picking up a a mountaineering magazine. "You mind?" he asked as he flipped it open. "I like to catch up each fall."

What a mystery. A renaissance man wrapped in fur. He'd just wooed her with plump oats, though she doubted wooing had been his intention. And that made him even more attractive.

Now he was reading. She sighed and picked up her mug. She held it in front of her body as if to protect herself from the vulnerability she felt as Rab unknowingly burrowed his way toward her heart.

No, not heart. This was lust. Lust for the yeti. She squirmed as she imagined rubbing her hands over his soft fur and hard muscles.

The coffee went down the wrong way. Helen sputtered and coughed, clearing her throat and trying to clear her mind.

"You okay?" Rab lurched forward as if to pat her back as she hacked the last of the coffee from her windpipe. But paper tore, ripped, his claws snagging on the magazine's cover as it slid from his lap. When his other hand shot out to grab the slippery pages, they speared the glossy paper. The tattered magazine fell to the floor, shreds dangling from Rab's claws.

It had to suck. She wasn't going to laugh. The look of utter frustration on his face made her heart go out to him. But her lips might have twitched. "Time for that manicure?"

A thrill went through her at the necessity of holding Rab's hands in hers during the process. Apparently, tamping down her attraction for him was not possible. She just wouldn't act on it. Helen had been faking it for a long time now, what was another month? At least at Toklat Lodge, her happiness was genuine.

———

RAB TRIED TWICE to put his hand into Helen's waiting palm and couldn't do it. She'd assembled her petite human nail clippers, a couple of nail files that looked like hot pink sandpaper on a stick, and his equipment: Top Dawg Dremel and Buster's Large Dog Nail Scissors.

"They just work better," he said, defending the uber embarrassing canine nail tools he kept in the lodge's storeroom. "If they made yeti claw care products, a lot of us would buy them. No one wants their toiletry kit furnished by Top Dawg. Except dogs, who don't care." He stole a glance at Helen. "Not that I know of. I mean, yeti aren't like pets or wild animals. We have fur, yeah, but some humans are really hairy too."

Helen reached across the table and gently took his hand in both of hers. "Rab. It's okay."

Humans blushed. He'd seen Helen turn a dozen shades of pink in the last twenty-four hours. It was so telling of her emotions. He imagined the extra blood flow now heating *his* cheeks might make him a little on the purple side instead of deep blue.

He didn't make a habit of talking claw care with other yeti, but it came up occasionally. Any yeti who lived like a human needed to trim their claws. Some yeti spent all day typing—like Tseten, who worked from his home as a computer programmer. Claws weren't practical for that kind of work.

But traditionally, yeti claws wore down from climbing rocks, biting them, or having their partners bite them as part of a mates' grooming practice. Claw care with a mate demonstrated trust. Rab had never trusted his claws to anyone else. Ever. Not until Helen. The significance of what she was about to do left him with a fluttering middle, even if she had no clue.

Letting her care for his claws seemed way more intimate than spooning against her body on the couch or the way they'd been flirting—something they should stop before it went any further. She had a life to go back to, and Rab valued the friendship they were building. Sex would complicate every-thing. He couldn't risk it.

Rab let his hand go limp in Helen's, ready for the process. "Okay," he said, looking away and closing his eyes. "I suggest the scissors, then the Dremel."

"We can wait," She said, her voice full of under-standing. "Or would you rather do this yourself?"

He let out a breath. He was being ridiculous. "No, this makes sense. It's awkward to cut claws on one hand while they're still long on the other, and then it's hard to cut with my right hand, since I'm left-handed," he explained. "It's just . . ."

She squeezed his hand. "I'm honored you're trusting me with this, Rab."

He finally met her gaze. Her tone held not a hint of teasing, and no laughter sparkled in her eyes. Only warmth. Caring. Patience. "Thank you for under-standing," he said, because Helen wasn't being flip-pant or cracking dog jokes or making light of his apprehension, and he appreciated that.

He settled his hand in hers. "I'm ready. Do your worst."

Her lips curved up before she bent to her task. "I intend to do my best."

Helen started with his pinky. It took some work for her to maneuver the nail scissors around the tip.

"I usually cut them in small increments," he told her. If she had a bad angle and tried to take too much off at once, the whole nail could shatter or bleed.

"Good idea." Her delicate brow furrowed. "I can see how it might be hard to get good leverage." She'd been holding the tool with one hand but added her other.

Rab felt a tug. Then with a snip, the tip of his claw flew off.

Helen gasped, glancing from his finger to the black piece of claw on the other side of the table. "Are you okay? Was that okay? The scissors slipped a little." She turned to him, her face stricken.

"It's fine," he said calmly. "Do that about a hundred more times, and I'll have short, non-lethal claws that will look like fingernails."

With a huff, Helen stood and came around the table. "Okay, but I'm going to try again while sitting next to you. A different position will help."

The chair next to Rab scraped against the polished wood flooring as Helen pulled it closer to him. She tried again and gasped as another quarter inch of claw sailed across the table. "I'm afraid I'm hurting you."

He was more concerned about the intimacy of what they were doing than the possibility of her hurting him physically. "Look, it hurts like a bitch to have a claw ripped out. But I don't think you'll do that or accidentally cut me to the quick."

Her face pinched in concentration. "I think I

need to cut from a different angle. Like tying someone else's tie, you know?"

"You mean a necktie? Uh, no. I don't know. I've never worn one."

"Some people can face a person and tie their tie for them. I've never been able to. I have to get behind the person as if I were tying my own tie." She chuckled. "Which makes no sense since I've never worn a necktie either."

"So, you need to stand behind me for this?"

She rubbed her forehead, considering. "I can't reach around you." Her cheeks flushed a beautiful shade of pink, like lingonberry blossoms in the spring. "What if I sit on your lap? My grip on the scissors and angle of execution would be better. I'd have more control and be less likely to hurt you."

Rab resisted a groan—of pleasure. He shouldn't want Helen on his lap. But he did, which was a problem if they were going to spend a platonic month together.

He pushed lusty thoughts out of his head. This wasn't Helen flirting. This was about getting a job done in the best way possible. He repeated that to himself several times. "Uh, sure," he said, affecting a casual tone. "If it gives you a better angle."

She pulled off her sweatshirt then straddled his thighs and held his hand in front of her.

She didn't weigh much, but the pressure of her body against his was sweet torture. Rab pictured slugs, worms, and maggots—unsexy things.

She wiggled her firm ass into his groin as she adjusted her position, and he tore his focus from the seductive angle of her smooth shoulder blades, closed his eyes, and drew a breath in through his nose.

Snip. Snip.

"Much better," Helen said, pulling his arm more firmly under her elbow and bending to her work.

With inches of claw to trim, it wasn't a quick exercise, but it took a hell of a lot less time than cutting them himself. And Rab eventually relaxed, so much so that, once she finished with the scissors and the Dremel, he didn't object to "touch up" work, which included a hot pink file, something called a buffer, and a clear coat of nail polish.

"This," Helen said, shaking the little bottle until the bead inside rattled, "will protect your claws. It blocks UV rays, so they won't turn yellow."

Rab cleared his throat. "My claws are black."

She rolled her eyes. "I'm sure it's still good for you."

This seemed like the kind of situation that warranted a simple nod. Did he want or need nail polish? No. Would it hurt anything to let Helen put it on his claws? Also, no.

Until she uncapped it.

He turned his face away from the fumes, frowning. The file and buffer had been fine, but . . . "It smells like paint. There's even a tiny paintbrush attached to the bottle cap. Humans use this to color their nails?"

She held her own hand up for his inspection. "Some do. Look." Her grin was contagious, and he gave in to her desire to varnish his claws.

It felt kind of nice, especially when she blew on his fingers, tickling him with her warm breath. Rab closed his eyes again until she finished, ending with the pinky on his left hand.

"All done." She tilted her head to survey her work. "I think they look great." She shifted to sit sideways in his lap, her smile dropping. "I mean, they look like human fingernails. Is that okay?"

It totally was. She'd tended to the job with more care than he ever had. Rab didn't need to, but he lifted his hand for inspection. "No more skewering olives," he said with a laugh. But winced as he noticed the bandage sticking out above the neckline of her shirt. His arm tightening around her as if to protect her from what he'd already done. "And no more scratching fellow caretakers."

She looked down at her chest. "Honestly, Rab. It's going to be fine. I probably didn't even need the bandage."

"Still, I'm sorry. I should have been more careful." Then he nodded toward his hands because he didn't want his eyes to stray anywhere else on her chest. "How long until these things are dry?"

"Oh, it dries really fast." She ran the pad of a finger over several of his nails. "Yep, all dry."

A beat passed. Why was Helen still sitting on his lap if she'd finished with his claws? Helen, who'd always been intriguing. Helen, who'd sketched his likeness from verbal descriptions and her imagination. Helen, who wasn't wearing a bra, and whose nipples poked the thin fabric of her shirt. Helen, who he lusted after. And Helen, who'd just trimmed his claws with all the care of a dedicated mate.

Her eyes grew wide as a heated charge built between them. Then she jumped off his lap, mumbled a few inconsequential pleasantries, and gathered her manicure tools before hurrying off to her room.

He stood and began sweeping up the shards of claw clippings, his chest aching. He'd let his thoughts get away from him. Helen had a future outside Toklat Lodge. She wouldn't want to hole up with a yeti for a mate, and Rab needed to remember that.

CHAPTER SIX

Helen knew they'd crossed an invisible line when she'd crawled onto Rab's lap and cared for his claws. The moment had felt incredibly intimate, though they hadn't discussed it.

During her first week at the lodge, they managed a delicate balance of civility and mutual respect, all while she tried to harness her attraction. But accidental touches set off sparks. Intentional touches lingered. And she was fairly sure Rab felt it too.

Helen's last sexual partner had been her ex, and that relationship had obviously ended horribly. All her friends back home were his friends too. Rab was the first friend she'd had in a long time that was all hers. She didn't want to jeopardize this precious and refreshing connection—no matter how much heat

Rab generated in her girly bits when they were together.

As it was, they were together a lot. They ate all their meals together, and spent long mornings at the breakfast table, sipping coffee and tea while reading. And they spent even longer evenings together at the Scrabble board or lounging on the couch—each at their respective ends. No more cuddling.

At her invitation, Rab joined Helen for yoga sessions. His flexibility surprised her.

They laughed. Helen smiled. Everything was more fun with Rab.

Her solo snowshoe trek that morning would also have been more fun if she'd invited him along. This was supposed to be The Month of Helen, her personal journey, but she'd focused mostly on Rab her first week at the lodge. More than once she'd had to restart a meditation session when she realized she'd been thinking about him.

And given the sexual tension whenever they were together, they needed space from one another—or a fire hose. By silent mutual agreement, they'd opted to spend time—not together—in the frosty winter air to cool their flaming libidos.

So while Helen strapped on snowshoes, Rab

fired up the snowblower, though arguably, they hadn't gotten enough new snow to blow.

She inhaled the refreshing midday air and pasted a serene smile on her face. If she acted calm and at peace, maybe she'd achieve it.

With that mindset, she imagined herself as a graceful, long-legged moose, gliding through the snow . . . and stumbled. Snowshoeing wasn't graceful, it was like wearing swim fins outside of a pool—awkward and hard work.

Clouds obscured the sun and mountains, but the day was beautiful in its own way. The air was still, and temperatures hovered right below freezing—warm for the time of year. Chickadee song filled the air as the birds flitted from branch to branch in the trees. And when she stopped moving, she heard the faint trickle of running water. Helen searched for and found the source—a small spring dribbling out of the hillside, creating a frozen fountain.

Rab would love it. Now she smiled for real. He'd also love the fat, little birds singing their cheerful songs. She wanted to bring him here. Share this with him.

She'd tell him about it later when they curled up with mugs of hot cocoa. They might be on opposite ends of the couch, but Rab didn't seem to mind when she wiggled her toes under his leg. Just to warm her feet. It wasn't flirting. His quads were massive, so he probably didn't even feel it. It wasn't an intimate touch or anything . . . even if the heat of him made her pulse race a little.

With her mind on Rab instead of her walk, Helen didn't see the tree stump, mostly buried by snow, until it snagged the toe of her snowshoe. She flew forward, arms outstretched to catch her fall. The frozen white stuff pelted her face in a stinging spray as she plowed down a slope through the powder.

She grabbed a branch, but her body didn't stop moving. Pain shot up her arm as the momentum wrenched her wrist into an unnatural position.

She came to a halt at the base of an alder, her snowshoes tangled in the tree limbs. She had a full load of snow down the back of her jacket, a cold, wet mess on her face, and a throbbing wrist. To add insult to injury, the upper branches of the alder unloaded, dumping more of the white stuff on her head.

Helen gasped for breath, wiping slushy snow from her face with her uninjured hand.

Shit.

She didn't think she'd broken it. Probably just a

sprain. But pain radiated to the tip of each finger when she rotated her injured hand. Not good.

Snowshoes. *Pfft.* They acted like giant snow shovels attached to each foot.

She rolled to her side, grumbling at the stump she'd tripped over as she cradled her wrist against her body.

But neither the snowshoes nor the stump were to blame. She'd been daydreaming instead of paying attention to her surroundings. The irony of the situation wasn't lost on her. She'd gone out alone to spend time by herself. However, she'd spent the entire hike thinking of Rab—to the point of distraction and injury.

Keeping Rab in the friendzone was proving harder than she'd expected. Could he be a friend and lover too? Or should she double down and rein in her urges before she did more than sprain her wrist?

RAB STARTED THE SNOWBLOWER. The two inches of light, dry snow didn't need to be cleared off the road-turned-winter-airstrip, but he needed to keep busy. He wasn't avoiding Helen—they spent most of each day together. He was giving her space, which felt rather like . . . well, avoiding her. And what better way to dodge someone than by running loud machinery. Blowing snow was not a two-person task.

Helen had come to the lodge on a personal journey, and Rab didn't want to get in her way. As it was, *her* yoga sessions had become *their* yoga sessions.

He liked her, respected her, and could barely control himself around her. He'd never been more attracted to anyone. She smelled like the tundra in the fall, filling him with comfort and a sense of returning home. He wanted to wrap his arms around her, bury his face in her dark hair, and never let go.

This was all very unsettling. Other yeti lived closer to human towns, had relationships with humans, and even held steady jobs in some circumstances. But he'd never considered such a lifestyle shift before meeting Helen.

His parents raised him to be nomadic. But it wasn't a lifestyle conducive to relationships—especially not with a human.

He was getting carried away. He would not make a move on Helen . . . unless she wanted him to. Because if she wanted him to . . .

He shook his head hard enough to rattle his teeth. She didn't. Her flirting had stopped right after the claw clipping—the most intimate experience he'd ever had.

He growled and pushed the blower into a deep drift. It put up a fight, which was exactly what he needed. He didn't care if it was a waste of time and energy to mow down one pile of snow only to create another right next to it. It was the only release he was likely to get.

CHAPTER SEVEN

"Longing," Rab said as he placed *ING* on the board. "That's nine points, plus a triple-word score, which makes it twenty-seven."

Helen sensed Rab studying her as she stared at her useless tiles. He was beating her soundly tonight. Her fingers tangled in her hair again. She rubbed at her scalp and let out a sigh.

"Something wrong?" he asked. "Need more tea? Or is it your wrist?" His hand slid across the table and stroked her fingers. Rab had done this several times since she'd injured her wrist several days earlier.

With every brush of his skin against hers, Helen's heart raced, even as the affectionate gesture soothed.

She almost wished she'd injured herself earlier to receive those caring caresses.

When she didn't reply he suggested, "Let's move so you can elevate your arm on the back of the couch."

She didn't want to move, didn't want him to stop touching her. But she admitted the real issue. "It's my hair. I tried to wash it yesterday, did a poor job of it with only one hand, and now the soap I couldn't rinse out is irritating my scalp. That's all." She shrugged.

His fingers stilled. "I can wash your hair."

"Right." Helen laughed because . . . he was joking, right? She looked up from the board game to see his serious expression. Her smile faded. "Oh, I . . ."

"In the kitchen sink," he hastened to clarify, lest she think he was implying they jump into the shower together. "I've done it before. A lot of the Denali guides live in dry cabins. When you don't have running water, you get creative. But the kitchen sink here even has a spray hose."

He didn't say he'd washed other women's hair, but it had to be what he meant. A jealous pang pulsed through her as she imagined those enormous hands tangled in another woman's locks.

She used her good hand to itch her head again. "The kitchen sink?" Oh, how she wanted to have clean hair. Why not take him up on his offer? She let out a huff then quirked a brow. "I guess you'd be returning the favor, right? I groomed your claws, and now you'd be grooming my hair?"

He looked at her, wide-eyed, his skin color deepening as he cleared his throat. "So, what do you say?"

She shivered, anticipating Rab's hands in her hair. When she spoke, her voice sounded husky, but she didn't care. "I say yes, please."

RAB PAWED through the bathroom cabinet in the Foraker Suite until he found bottles of mint-scented herbal shampoo and conditioner. He knew nothing about women's toiletries or what fragrance Helen would select for herself, but she'd left it up to him. The scents were clean. Refreshing. Relaxing. All sensations he wanted to impart to her.

His desire to run his hands through her long, dark-as-a-December-night hair and see the contrast against his short, white fur was beside the point. This was about her.

His stride faltered when he returned to the

kitchen. Helen smiled, wide and full of appreciation. But what tripped him up was her top—or lack thereof.

She wore another of her thin, sleeveless under-shirts. He loved them. Tight and low cut, often showing a lot of bra, the full roundness of her breasts, and the two red marks left by his claws. They triggered something possessive and primal in him.

Tonight, she wasn't wearing a bra. Her breasts stretched the fabric, nipples pressing into the cloth. He focused on the deep *V* of her cleavage like a drooling grizzly ready to pounce above a pika hole. He wanted to explore. Wanted to kiss his way along the edge of the fabric and pull it lower to reveal what he'd seen when she'd been in the hot tub.

"Did you find the shampoo you were looking for?" She seemed oblivious to the lusty thoughts running through his head.

He snapped his gaze to hers and held up the bottles. "Sure did," he said as he tried to scour the image of Helen's gorgeous tits from his mind.

They placed a towel across the front of the counter for padding. She bent forward, head and hair hanging in the sink, good arm providing support beneath her chest. Her yoga pants hugged her round, pert ass. "Like this?" she asked, her voice echoing in the sink.

He gritted his teeth and fought back a groan as he began to stir. "Yep, just like that." He looked down. He was way too turned on. "I'm just going to grab an apron."

She huffed a laugh. "Sorry, Rab. We might both get wet. It's why I took off my shirt."

He gave Helen a noncommittal hum in response and tied the apron securely around his waist—in part to keep his clothes dry but mostly to cover his inevitable boner.

She needed this. Her irritated scalp itched. This was not about his pleasure, but hers.

Rab reached around Helen, his front brushing her backside as he grabbed the spray hose. "Excuse me," he said.

She laughed and wiggled her hips. "Am I in the way? Let me know if I need to move."

He let out a breath and touched a hand to her shoulder. "You're perfect. Ready for the water?"

"Yes." Her voice was low, husky. It must have been the acoustics with her head in the sink.

He checked the water temperature, then held the nozzle against her hairline, slowly running the spray up the back of her head. He repeated this movement until he'd thoroughly soaked her hair.

The scent of the herb-mint shampoo wafted up as he worked a lather between his palms. Blue fingers disappeared into dark, glossy strands as he gently massaged it in, rubbing his fingertips, with their neatly trimmed claws, against her scalp.

When he ran his thumbs up the base of her skull, Helen let out a moan. His name tumbled from her lips. "Rab," she groaned, "that feels so good."

Rab's heart raced. He was grooming her like a mate . . . pleasing her. But he enjoyed it too, and his *Go Kiss a Moose* apron didn't hide a thing.

HELEN WAS WET. And not only her hair. Rab's massaging hands were foreplay as far as her body was concerned. He had to know what he was doing. He could have washed her hair quickly and efficiently. Instead, he'd opted for slow and sensual. She loved it.

With every pass of his fingers, she let out an involuntary murmur. Rab would grunt in response, his hard body lightly rubbing against hers. Never a satisfying grind. Just a hint of pressure. A chance encounter. Always elusive. She would subtly move her hips, searching for his—a pleasure point that teased and moved.

"I love the scent," she purred as he worked the conditioner through her hair. He'd turned her into a limp noodle against the kitchen counter. "Thank you. It's perfect."

Rab let out another rumble, and his hips teased hers as he leaned in.

Maybe she needed to praise him to get more contact. Did she *want* more contact? Yes. No. *Gah!* Helen wanted Rab, no doubt. But she also wanted a friend. And he was a yeti. Could they even have sex? Was that a thing? Was it weird? The idea of it didn't feel weird. He was washing her hair. No human guys she knew would do that.

She adjusted her stance again until she made full contact, her backside against Rab's front. His warmth and hardness as he leaned into her made her shiver. When he let out a sound—part groan and part growl —it vibrated through him into her. For a moment, their hips found a slow, subtle rhythm as his hands worked magic. When he ran his thumbs down her neck, she expected his wet touch to sizzle on contact with her hot skin.

He pulled away, and they were both silent as he

ran the water along her scalp in smooth, even passes to rinse the conditioner from her hair.

Finally, he leaned in, and she heard the spray hose retract. Then he slid his palms over her head, squeezing water out of her long tresses.

Helen's body thrummed with desire. But should she acknowledge it? Clearly Rab was just as turned on, but she didn't know his intentions. Which prospect made her more nervous—that Rab might be into it or that he might reject her? She didn't want to mess this up.

After he stepped aside, she worked the last drops of water out of her hair with her good hand, and he helped her wrap her hair in the towel she'd been leaning against. With a contented sigh, she flipped her towel-clad head up and peered at Rab. His face was darker than normal, eyelids at half-mast.

She let out a long breath and tried for some middle ground. "That felt so good." She'd let him determine if she meant the hair washing or his body pressing against hers. Because both were awesome.

Rab grunted and pulled the spray hose out again to rinse the sink.

Helen couldn't read him, but before she over-thought it, she reached for the yeti and gave him a side hug. Friends hugged. That was a thing. Rab's solid muscle and soft fur made her want to purr and rub the side of her face in it, but she forced herself to pull back. "I owe you."

His arm wound loosely around her. "Never," he said. "My pleasure."

Pleasure, god yes. "Mine too." She focused on his full, indigo lips. How would they feel against hers? And the fur on his cheeks? Would it scratch, leaving a sweet burn on her skin? "Thank you," she whispered. His lips were closer now. His hand firm on her back.

Were they going to kiss? One kiss wouldn't mess things up between them, would it? Because lip-on-lip action seemed inevitable. Her tongue darted out to wet her lips, readying for him. His breath whispered soft and warm on her face.

A jet of water shot between them. Rab yelled, and Helen jumped back.

"Shit. Sorry." He looked at the hose in his hand like he didn't understand where the water had come from. "Is your wrist okay?"

She lifted her injured arm, her wrist wrapped in a damp bandage. "I'm fine," she said. True. And yet, also not. The spray hose had either saved or cockblocked them from acting on this magnetic pull. Either way, the moment was gone. She took it as a sign and moved another step away from the deliciously hot yeti. "I think it's time to dry my hair and go to bed. Goodnight, Rab."

CHAPTER EIGHT

Helen had struggled to keep her hands to herself the first two weeks at the lodge, but the third week was torture. Even the impending trip to Denali for the Halloween party, where she'd meet some of Rab's friends, didn't distract her from the lust that had consumed her since sexy-hair-washing night.

She washed her own hair midweek. If Rab had run his hands through her hair or ground himself against her again, she would not have been able to hold back, despite wanting to keep him as a friend.

Fitful nights did nothing to douse her desire for him. She'd wake up just as horny. Her X-rated dreams all starred Rab and what she wanted to do to him—holding his erection in her hands, running her tongue along his length, and taking him into her wet, willing body.

She muffled a frustrated cry with a pillow. But even through layers of down, she smelled coffee. Mornings with Rab were the best. If only she didn't want to rip off her clothes and rub her breasts against his furry chest.

Helen decided to go down to breakfast in her ankle-length, flannel nightgown with its high-buttoned collar. It was warm, matronly, and sure to function as a chastity belt. She pulled on wool socks and a Toklat Lodge terry cloth robe for good measure —the very definition of unsexy.

Calling, "Morning, Rab," she entered the dining room with her e-reader. "How'd you sleep?"

He'd just set a pot of coffee at her spot. "Like a fly-bitten caribou in a cloud of mosquitoes," he muttered as he went to get the rest of their breakfast.

When he returned, she asked, "Not like a baby mountain goat in a soft patch of clover?"

He shook his head as he set a plate of pilot bread on the table. "No. *And* I burned our breakfast. So now it's crackers and jam."

"Crackers are fine." She sat across from him and filled his teacup. He looked as bad off as she felt. Wrinkles creased his flannel shirt, and his collar appeared higher on one side because he'd done up his shirt wrong. "Dale might come today. Aren't you excited about the party?"

She'd been mulling over the fact that she and Rab would no longer be alone once Dale arrived to pick them up. She'd have to share Rab with others for the first time. The prospect should have relieved her but was strangely upsetting instead. She enjoyed having him to herself.

He grunted again. "I am," he said, though his tone did not agree. "And we'll find a costume for you."

"Think Dale would outfit me as a mountain climber from the last century? He has all the clothes in his closet." And since she was on the topic, she nodded at his chest. "I think you missed a button."

He grinned at her comment about Dale's clothing, then looked down at his shirt and rolled his eyes before starting to undo them. At her wide yawn, he asked, "How'd *you* sleep?"

"Also like a caribou in mosquito season—I think. Anyway, I slept poorly."

Rab looked at her, concern etching his face. "Is it your wrist? I thought it was healing."

"Not my wrist, it's getting better." She didn't want to admit what had really kept her up—a hot, burning desire for him—especially not when his shirt gapped, displaying sexy, muscular yeti chest. So she left it at that and took a sip from her mug.

Rab made the best coffee. But today it tasted bitter. He was off. They both were.

Despite her assurance, he didn't let her injury drop. He reached out and slid his fingers over hers, his thumb lightly rubbing her palm.

Goose bumps shot up her arm. Her nipples went hard as his fingers brushed across the inside of her wrist. Could he make her orgasm with that touch alone?

Rab's glacier-blue gaze grew intent. His nostrils flared. The lustful look he gave her made her flush from head to toe. Did he smell her arousal? The idea made her even wetter.

She bit her lip, watching his fingers caress her. "Your touch feels right." Her eyes fluttered shut.

He growled her name. It was a good growl. Sexy. It made her already hard nipples stand out like the granite peaks of the Alaska Range. Rab stood and rounded the table, his shirt still wide open above his jeans. He placed a hand on her armrest and swiveled her chair to face him.

Her breaths came in short bursts. So did his.

He crouched in front of her, eyes like blue

flames. "Helen," he rumbled as he ran a hand up her flannel-covered calf.

She spread her legs in invitation, and he inhaled again and shivered. Because of her. She did this to him.

"I want you," he growled. "Do you want this?"

"Yes." She wanted it. Badly. Although uncertain what he would do, she trusted Rab. She moaned and shifted to make more room for the yeti between her legs.

He moved to her ankles, sliding the backs of his fingers up to meet the top of her socks and bare legs.

Under her nightgown, he stroked her thighs. His soft fur tickling as the smooth pads of his fingers circled closer and closer to her core. She let out a low whimper when his fingers glided over the fabric of her panties.

"You *are* wet," he said with another growl.

Helen bit her lip and nodded. Drenched. Weeks of sexual tension and months of nothing but self-pleasure had primed her for Rab's touch. She lifted her ass so he could pull her panties off.

Rab handed them to her, then dove headfirst under her nightgown, his broad shoulders spreading her wide.

Helen squealed, gripping his head where it

nestled under the flannel between her legs. The nightgown wasn't an effective chastity belt after all. *Thank god.*

His soft fur teased the length of her inner thighs, brushing against her most sensitive places. Then his fingers were on her, stroking, opening her folds. He paused, and she felt his breath on her center before his long, broad tongue lapped at her. Helen arched her body and nearly came. "Holy fuck!" She gripped the edge of the table with one hand, her other hand holding steady on Rab's head through the fabric of her nightgown. "Oh . . . yes!"

He cradled her ass in both hands and slid her forward, tipping her up against his mouth so his wet, textured tongue could move faster over her nub. Helen saw stars. When one large, manicured finger slid inside her, she gasped. Her legs shook uncontrollably as she clenched around it. She was vaguely aware of pressing herself hard against him as her orgasm peaked. Rab's name tumbled from her lips as she broke apart on his tongue.

Eyes clenched shut in pleasure, she collapsed back against the chair as he slid his hand from under her. He gave her sex one final lick, a tender caress. She shivered at the loss of his warmth as he withdrew and straightened the flannel around her legs.

Through the haze of her intense orgasm, she heard a low and persistent whine. A plane.

Rab kissed her forehead, and her eyes blinked open. "Dale's here," he said as he turned from her.

Helen forced herself to sit up. What the fuck had just happened? She'd never had such an intense orgasm. Her body was like rubber.

She watched in a daze as he strode across the room. "Wait, where are you going?"

"My room," Rab called as he disappeared.

She moved to scrub a hand across her face to bring herself back from Pleasureland, but she was still clutching her underwear and scratched her cheek with the lace. She wanted to follow Rab and continue what they'd just started. Didn't he want that too? Why had he gone to his room? Because of the approaching plane?

She pushed to her feet and made her way to her own room on shaky legs. She had to get ready to meet people and attend a Halloween party.

Helen sighed. She did not want to share her yeti.

Whoa. Her yeti? He *had* just rocked her world, but did that make him hers? She and Rab had gone from fun and flirtation to finger fucking.

Hers or not, she desperately wanted more.

RAB'S DICK pressed uncomfortably against his jeans, causing him to walk stiffly as he hurried back to his suite. He closed the door and undid his fly, giving himself a stroke. He groaned.

Helen had been so wet. So willing. He wanted to be with her now. His body shook with desire, and he licked his lips, tasting her. Her sweet, musky scent coated his beard. The realization almost made him come where he stood.

He shucked off his clothes and crossed to the bathroom in quick, urgent strides to turn on the shower. But he didn't duck immediately under the spray. He wasn't ready to wash her scent off. Instead, he gripped his dick harder, sliding his hand up and down as he remembered her sweet, swollen folds, her moans of pleasure. The way she'd gripped his head, riding his finger and tongue as she'd broken apart. The way she'd called his name at the height of her climax. Rab's muscles tightened, his orgasm pulsing through him as he spent himself on the shower wall.

With a sigh, Rab slid under the spray. He braced his hands on the tile to steady himself as the water rushed over him.

He drew in one deep breath, then another, until his head cleared.

What the hell have I done? To get her off on his tongue and fingers was one thing. But he wanted to slide his throbbing blue dick inside her sweet, wet heat, which might have happened if the plane hadn't been on approach.

Is Dale's timing horrible, or should I be thankful? It's not like Rab hadn't been with women, but this was Helen. The interruption made him second guess where he and Helen were headed. Doubt crept in. Other women had slept with him, satisfied their curiosity, and he'd never seen them again. He didn't want that to happen with Helen. His chest ached at the thought. He hoped to hell she didn't regret it, because it had been the most incredible experience of Rab's life.

CHAPTER NINE

I t took a full hour for Helen's cheeks to lose their post-orgasmic flush—about the amount of time it took her to shower and finishing packing. But as she joined Rab and Dale in the lodge's dining room, they heated again when her eyes met Rab's.

"H-hi," she managed, voice breathless and body tingling as she recalled what they'd done in this very room.

She managed to tear her gaze away from the yeti when Dale cheerfully responded, "Howdy, sunshine," before taking a sip from his coffee mug. He sat at the table, legs crossed like he was catching up with an old friend. Because he and Rab were old friends—right.

She frowned, and her hands curled into fists as she narrowed her focus on Dale. "Howdy yourself."

Dale's smile faltered, and his eyes slid from Helen to Rab and back as if he had no idea why she might be upset.

She'd messaged Dale about Rab's presence, but thought she'd wait to give him a piece of her mind till they were in person. She let loose now. "All this time, you knew about yeti, and you didn't tell me? You dropped me off at this remote lodge, knowing your regular caretaker, a yeti, might show up to work *his* job. And. You. Didn't. Tell. Me."

Dale's dark eyes met hers, and he shrugged, relaxed as ever. "I didn't think Rab would be here. But he's a good guy. Looks like you two have gotten along fine."

Did Dale suspect just how well she and Rab had gotten along? The pilot seemed oblivious, but heat pricked up her neck. Would he judge her if he knew? Did she care?

Dale continued, "Besides, it isn't my secret to tell. You'll have to keep the yeti secret too when you leave."

Her breath caught at the reminder of her return ticket, and her gaze landed on Rab, who'd been silently rotating the teacup in his large hands. She didn't want to think about leaving, especially after what had happened between them that morning.

"Of course I'll keep the secret," she said, unable to meet Rab's eyes. Instead, she stared at those large, careful hands holding the delicate cup.

Crap, I knew this would happen. He went down on me, and things immediately became complicated. She'd been so focused on trying to dampen the sexual energy between them, she hadn't considered what an actual relationship with a yeti might look like. Could they go on dates? What would she tell her friends? Or her mother?

She and Rab needed to talk. Maybe once they arrived at Dale's house in Denali, they could go for an after-dinner walk, regardless of the dark or the frigid temperature. Otherwise, they might not have a moment alone all weekend.

Dale slurped his coffee. "I've spent a long time in these parts and have known about yeti my whole life."

"Dale's family—he and his brother—have always been yeti-friendly," Rab added.

"I didn't realize you had a brother, Dale," Helen said before shaking her head. "I grew up around here too. What does *yeti-friendly* even mean?"

"You grew up in Fairbanks," Dale clarified.

Evidently, Alaska's second largest city was too metropolitan for its residents to understand what actually went on in the wilds of Alaska.

It irked. She knew how to dress a moose and could start a fire in any weather, even during a raging blizzard.

And in her heart, she'd always believed in yeti. She just hadn't seen one. Until meeting Rab.

"We call humans who employ or otherwise help us and keep us secret *yeti-friendly*," Rab explained. "Like Dale or Mountain High Guiding Service."

Dale shrugged. "There's even a law firm in Anchorage helping yeti obtain property."

This piqued her professional interest. "Really?"

Rab nodded. "Creer and Associates. They helped Tseten acquire his land and home." He turned to Dale. "Is he coming to the party?"

Dale chuckled. "Tseten miss a party? He's driving up with Pema and invited everyone he knows."

"He doesn't actually know many people since he's a yeti." Rab clarified for Helen's benefit. "Pema's his cousin, and also a yeti. She's a caterer and makes the best momos—Tibetan dumplings." He kissed his fingers in appreciation.

Dale nodded in agreement. "They are delicious."

Helen tried her best not to show her surprise that any yeti owned their own homes. "Where's his house?"

"The Chugach—outside of Anchorage," Dale replied.

Rab cleared his throat. "Not all yeti are nomadic."

A subtle reminder of how different they were. They really needed to have that talk.

Dale drained his mug. "Ready to go? It's a perfect day for a flight to Denali. The mountain is out," he said, referring to the town's namesake peak.

They were soon airborne with the lodge, their haven, disappearing behind them.

Helen tried to focus on the frosted beauty of the Alaska Range and Dale's easygoing commentary about the landscape below them. She usually loved it. Today, her mind wouldn't focus on anything but the morning activities with the yeti who now sat silently behind her.

RAB COULDN'T SHAKE the doubt that had crept in after getting himself off to memories of Helen coming against his tongue and her sweet, musky scent. He needed time to think, and being in Denali would give him a little breathing room, what with the party and all the people. Okay, not that many people, but after spending months alone and weeks with only Helen, three was a crowd. And tomorrow, when Tseten and crew arrived, it would be an all-out circus.

He lay on the drafty floor of Dale's cabin, listening to Helen's soft breathing mere feet away as she slept on the couch. She was so close, yet never farther away. Even though they'd shared such intimacy that morning, she'd be gone in a little more than a week. At the thought, his heart did something it had never done before for any other person. It ached.

He wanted to sleep on the couch with her wrapped in his arms. But Helen hadn't made any affectionate overtures toward him since that morning in the dining room. No light touch of her hand against his arm, no accidental brush against him.

Message received, loud and clear—she didn't want anyone to know. And with the way his heart continued to burn in his chest, it was probably a good thing Dale had arrived when he had.

The air mattress squeaked and groaned as Rab turned to face the wall, forcing his eyes to shut and his mind to move on. He didn't know many people, but most of them would be at this party, a highlight of his solitary life. And he'd enjoy it, damn it, even if his heart was preoccupied with the obsidian-haired beauty who'd most definitely changed his life.

CHAPTER TEN

Helen had never felt lonelier than she did with Rab curled up mere feet away.

Earlier that evening, when she'd suggested they go for a walk, Dale overheard and assumed it was a general invitation. Rab hadn't protested, either not realizing her intention or not wanting to talk.

She dozed, tossing and turning—not that Dale's old couch afforded much room for restlessness—until the early hours of the morning when she finally drifted off to a guided meditation recording. Then she slept hard.

A honking horn yanked her from a deep slumber. Groggily she sat up and rubbed her eyes open. Rab and Dale were peering out the front window as gray morning light filtered in around them.

The light meant it was midmorning already. Helen yawned. "What time is it?" She peeled back her borrowed sleeping bag, pulled on thick socks over her leggings, and slid her arms into a fleece jacket.

"Nearly eleven, sunshine. Coffee?" Dale greeted her.

"Y-yes," she responded on another yawn as she padded to the window. Dale shuffled into the kitchen, as she came up alongside Rab. She ached to lean into him, rest her sleepy head against the soft T-shirt covering his warm chest and encircle his middle with her arms. But he'd been distant since yesterday, so she left space between them. "Good morning. You guys let me sleep in."

"Morning," Rab rumbled, then said, "You looked as snug as a winter hare in a warren. Didn't want to disturb you."

Her lips quirked into a smile as she looked up into warm blue eyes. She reached for him then, her hand nearly touching the fur on his forearm, when Dale returned from the kitchen.

"Cream or sugar?" he asked, passing her a steaming cup.

She thanked Dale and declined both as she wrapped her hands around the vintage mug instead of Rab's soft arm. While she sipped, her gaze slid from Rab to an RV in the driveway. Then she sputtered. "There's a yeti driving that camper."

"Tseten," Rab responded, as if that was answer enough. "Did an eighteen-point turn to get that boat angled right."

Dale rejoined them at the window. "He'll be glad to meet you."

A low vibration came from Rab. He patted his chest and coughed.

She gave him a curious side-eye. It sounded like he'd growled. "I'm eager to meet your friends, but why would Tseten be glad to meet me?" Humans, unlike yeti, were common.

"Since you now know about yeti, you're one more person he can add to his social pool," Rab explained.

The camper door opened, and large bodies tumbled out like clowns from a Volkswagen Bug.

Tseten reached the front door first, knocking as he let himself in. "The party has arrived," he boomed, arms open wide. Aside from his fur and blue skin, he looked like a model for an outdoor clothing company in his hiking pants and light weight puffy jacket. Compared to Rab, his eyes were lighter in color and facial fur more neatly trimmed.

The others stomped their boots on the porch to

release snow then shuffled in behind him. A female yeti, who must have been Tseten's cousin Pema, rolled her eyes at his proclamation. "Because Tset *is* the party," she said with more than a hint of sarcasm.

"Who rented a camper to travel to a Halloween bash?" Tseten asked.

"Me." A dark-haired woman traveling with the group raised her hand and quirked a smile. "Technically I did. It's my name and driver's license on the contract."

Another yeti passed through the front door. He readjusted his trucker-style Mountain High Guiding Service hat as he added, "And don't forget the deposit is on the company card. You all need to do exactly as Toni says when it comes to the RV antifreeze that the camper's water system requires. We're bound by the rental agreement."

Tseten raised his arms in defense. "I'm not going to jack up the plumbing."

Pema raised an eyebrow and nodded back toward a blond man—approximately the size and coloring of Thor—exiting the camper. "Tell that to Eddie." Her snickering stopped a moment later when her gaze landed on Helen. Pema froze, her eyes wide and flawless royal-blue skin tightening over smooth, defined cheekbones as she frowned. Evidently *Pema* was not happy to meet Helen.

But Tseten's eyes lit, and his smile broadened—as predicted. He came toward Helen with outstretched arms, and his giant yeti mitts swallowed her hand in greeting. "You must be Helen. I've heard so much about you."

"Y-you have?" She glanced at Rab. He shrugged and flicked his eyes to Dale.

The brunette stepped forward. "Don't worry. Tseten has heard something about everyone." She offered a quick handshake. "I'm Toni. We understand you had a mix-up with this guy here." She tilted her head to indicate Rab, then gave him a hug. "So nice to see you, Rabten. It's been a while."

During their time at the lodge, Helen had given little thought to his interactions with others, specifically other women. Toni seemed friendly, but Helen felt a prick of jealousy when Rab wrapped an arm around Toni, even if only briefly.

"Dale booked two caretakers," Rab told the group. "Helen and I arrived on the same day."

Toni glanced back to Helen. "Did you know about yeti before Dale introduced you?"

"Dale didn't exactly introduce us," Helen began,

her gaze meeting Rab's. Was he recalling their "meeting"? Or was that just wishful thinking?

Dale tossed up his hands. "I dropped Helen at the lodge. Didn't know Rab was already there sleeping. He and Helen bumped into each other after I left."

Toni's hand went to her mouth as she looked back and forth between Dale, Helen, and Rab. "Oh my god, Dale. You left her nearly a hundred miles off the road system, at a remote lodge, where she assumed she was alone. Then she discovered she was sharing the place with a *yeti*? And she had no idea they existed. Holy shit!"

Dale shrugged and muttered something about doing his best.

Rab's big, warm hand slid around Helen's. "Yes, we met and agreed the lodge was big enough for two. End of story."

No one commented. They were too busy staring at Rab and Helen's joined hands, and probably assuming there was a lot more to the story.

As if suddenly realizing how it looked, Rab dropped her hand. "Let me make introductions." He gestured to Tseten. "You've already met this guy. Everyone here, except Tset, works for Mountain High Guiding Service in some capacity. Tseten owns and operates Chugach Programming. Nice guy but chattier than a magpie."

Tseten frowned. "You say that like it's a bad thing, but it's not like we have an online yeti forum. You all love my news." Several shoulders begrudgingly shrugged, and Helen bit back a smile. Most people liked gossip when it wasn't about them.

Rab continued introductions, gesturing to the female yeti. "This is Pema. She and Tseten are cousins. Pema makes the best dumplings in all of Alaska and sells them through her catering company, Blue Lotus. She also moonlights as an accountant for Mountain High."

Pema still looked like she had her doubts about Helen.

He moved on to the yeti with the trucker hat. "Denzin is the regional manager for Mountain High, and my boss when I'm guiding."

Steel-blue eyes regarded her as Denzin gave her hand a quick, firm shake.

"You met Toni," Rab said, gesturing to the friendly, dark-haired woman. "She works in Mountain High's Wildwood office." Next he turned to the Norse god doppelgänger. "And this is Eddie. He's a guide and sometimes office manager at Mountain

High's Palmer office. And he may or may not have jacked up the RV's plumbing."

Eddie tucked a strand of golden hair behind his ear. "I didn't touch the plumbing. I claimed my bed in the camper."

Voices erupted as everyone had something to say about the limited bed space. Yeti were big. Sharing beds would be challenging.

While the others squabbled, Denzin handed Rab a thick white envelope. The light seemed to dim in Denzin's eyes. "Wedding invitation. My brother's getting married over Thanksgiving. He asked me to pass this along."

Rab's eyes widened as he read through the invite, and Toni gave Denzin's arm a supportive squeeze. Clearly there was more to this story too.

"I hope you can make it. Of course, you're welcome to bring Helen," Denzin offered.

Heat ignited across Helen's cheeks. Did they think she and Rab were an item? Aside from holding her hand in front of everyone, he'd been keeping his distance. "Thank you," she said, "but I'm only in Alaska another week. My best to your brother and his bride—or groom." She tried for a warm smile. "Whomever he's marrying."

Helen excused herself. A room full of Rab's

friends left her overwhelmed after weeks of virtual solitude. She hadn't even been to the bathroom yet since waking up, and she needed a moment alone to sort through her thoughts while she finished her much-needed coffee.

She wouldn't have blushed if she didn't have confused feelings for Rab. A small thrill had run through her at the thought of being his date, and at Denzin's *assumption* that *Helen* would be at Rab's side. But she'd be leaving soon. So, how should she feel about the yeti? And more important, how did he feel about her?

RAB SILENTLY CURSED himself as Helen, glossy hair still wild from sleep, walked away from him and Denzin.

His friend motioned toward her retreating back. "Apologies. Did I misread the situation? I'm good at that." He glanced at the invitation.

Rab shook his head. "No, no worries, Zin. Helen's stay has always been temporary." He also eyed the gold, embossed invitation. Denzin's half-brother was human—they shared the same human father. And apparently, the brother was marrying

Denzin's ex-girlfriend, also human. Rab wanted to tell his friend he was better off without the woman. But he was so conflicted about himself and Helen, he had no business offering advice.

"Thank your brother for the invite. If weather permits, I'll be there. No plus one."

While Denzin turned back to the group, Rab moved to the couch to tidy up Helen's bedding so others could sit. He paused when her scent hit him and had to resist the urge to bury his face in her sleeping bag. He forced himself to stuff it down into its storage sack. Then he flopped onto the couch while the others continued to debate sleeping arrangements.

Why had he taken Helen's hand in front of everyone, as if there were something between them? A little fooling around did not equal a relationship. He'd been surprised by the stab of jealousy he'd felt at Tseten's eager greeting, even if the guy's intentions were one hundred percent platonic.

He needed to chill the fuck out and keep his distance. He'd do well to follow Helen's cues—they just weren't telling him what his heart wanted to hear. She was distancing herself, leaving.

CHAPTER ELEVEN

H elen tugged at the low bodice of her borrowed costume and searched the crowd for Rab.

The legendary Halloween party took place in a four-bedroom house owned by a climbing guide who rented rooms to seasonal workers at Denali National Park. In typical Alaska style, the house was formerly a one-room cabin with several additions that included bedrooms, a modern kitchen, and a garage large enough to store an RV.

At least fifty partygoers packed the place, spilling outside to a huge bonfire that lit up the night. Given the remoteness of Denali in winter, it was an impressive turnout.

Winding her way through the crush inside,

Helen felt the thumping bass in her chest like a heartbeat. Given the number of people present, she had little hope of getting any alone time with Rab, but that didn't stop her from searching for him.

A small-town Alaska house party wasn't so different from one in the Lower Forty-Eight. But Alaskans were way more creative about using what they had around the house for costumes. For instance, underwear worn over long johns made an acceptable superhero costume. One woman had a Ruth Bader Ginsburg bun, a black shirt, and a lace collar that looked like it had been a foam packing sleeve for a pear in a former life.

Dale hadn't been keen on loaning her his clothes to use as a costume. And Rab's friends hadn't offered anything so simple as a red cape and devil horns. Oh no. Instead, Helen wore a zebra-striped bodice, a deer antler headband, and cat whiskers on her cheeks. She was a freakin' sexy zedeercat . . . in fishnets. And on top of all that, the bodice cut so low it exposed the ends of her now-healed claw scratches.

But she could hardly care what she wore or what others might make of the marks. Her jumbled feelings focused more on Rab who seemed to be avoiding her.

Helen passed Toni and Pema. Toni sported

Princess Lea buns and a white robe. Pema comple-
mented Tseten's Viking costume with her own
Valkyrie bodice, cape, and shield. Both Rab and
Denzin had "dressed" as Wookiees, though Denzin
refused to attend without pants. Rab didn't seem
phased by going nude.

Helen almost asked Toni and Pema if they'd seen
Rab, but she let them go by without a word. She
didn't want them wondering about her motives.

She and Rab needed to talk about what had
happened back at the lodge. The truth was that every
time she thought back to his mouth on her goodies,
she got wet all over again. She might be leaving in a
week, and her emotions might be in a jumble, but
Helen was horny . . . and she missed Rab.

She squeezed into the next room, lifting her
drink so a guy in a blue plastic storage drum—
commonly used in rural Alaska for everything from
food to fuel—could squeeze by. She couldn't help
smiling as she noted his drum swung from rainbow
suspenders.

Her smile faltered when she spotted Rab leaning
against the far wall, one leg crossed over the other, as he
sipped a beer and casually chatted with two women she
hadn't seen before. She tried to squash another pang of
jealousy. For someone who lived in the woods for half

the year, he sure knew a lot of people. And a too-high proportion, in her opinion, seemed to be women.

He towered over everyone, yet he didn't stand out. With the bandolier, he did look like a Wookiee. Except instead of matted brown fur, his was white and fluffy.

Some people clearly knew him. He got fist bumps and pats on the back. But others complimented his amazing costume, having no clue he was actually naked.

With a hollow ache in her stomach, she watched as he smiled at the two women. His real smile—when his eyes crinkled in the corners. The woman in the witch hat curled her finger at him, beckoning him close. Except instead of whispering in Rab's ear, she placed her hands on his cheeks and pressed her lips to his.

Helen's pulse whooshed in her ears, but she couldn't tear her eyes away. How many times had she imagined those lips on hers in a tender kiss?

Rab looked up just then, and his eyes locked with Helen's. She spun around. Maybe he wouldn't know she'd been staring. Longing.

She crashed into the back of a guy in a Hawaiian shirt.

The man slowly turned around, ogling her chest before looking her in the eye. His brown eyes, dark hair, and big fake mustache contrasted with his pale skin. He feigned indignation. "You realize you just spilled beer on Magnum P.I.?"

Helen tried to place his accent. "Sorry about the beer, Magnum." She eyed his bright top, covered with gaudy pineapples and palm trees. The character from the popular show in the 1980s would have never worn such a print. "Uh, nice shirt." She looked down. "And short shorts." This guy was not afraid to show some pale Alaskan leg.

He raised his cup in salute before taking Helen's hand and kissing her knuckles. His lips were cold. Still bent over her hand, he looked up at her with passion in his eyes. "I'm Antonio. And your name, *mi amor?*"

"H-Helen," she said, showing her agitation as she stumbled over her own name. She didn't want to talk to Antonio. She wanted Rab . . . to be the one locking lips with him.

"Helen. May I call you Helena?" He didn't wait for her to respond. *"Eras tan preciosa,* Helena." He still held her hand in his cold grip as his gaze dipped back to her chest. "What do we have here? A striped deer? No, you have whiskers. A black-and-white leopard? No, you have antlers."

As Helen started to answer, a furry arm slid possessively around her shoulders.

"She's with me, bloodsucker." Rab's low rumble sounded almost threatening.

Storm clouds passed over Antonio's face. His lip curled as he looked up at Rab. "Really? How *abominable* for her."

Rab's body tensed, and she felt a low growl reverberate between their bodies.

What the hell was going on? She'd never had men fight over her. She attracted the kind who made commitments and then broke them. At least, her ex had.

Rab spun her around and guided her through the crowd, which parted readily for him. He ushered her down a hall and into a bedroom.

Two women were making out on the bed. They broke apart with a startled "Fuck!" and "What the hell?" but went silent when they spotted Rab.

"Is this your room?" he asked through clenched teeth.

They glared but shook their heads, and he gestured to the door. "Then please feel free to continue elsewhere."

He shut the door behind them.

Helen spun away from his hold, hands on her hips. "What's your problem, Rab?"

"My problem? I'm not the one who was kissing a vampire."

"He was dressed as Magnum P.I., not a vampire." Helen's chest heaved with annoyance. How dare he? "Besides, you should talk. *He* kissed my *hand*." She waved an arm toward the door and the masses beyond. "You had a witch locked to your *lips*."

Rab's eyes widened as she spoke. He stepped forward, placing his hands over her cleavage as if covering it. "She kissed *me*, and she did so without my permission," he said in a low voice.

Helen gave him a hard look, her gaze traveling from his eyes to where his hands covered her chest. "Did I give *you* permission to touch *me*?"

He looked stricken. "No, you didn't. But your tit popped out when you gestured about the witch." He squeezed his eyes shut and began to move his hands away.

Helen caught them and held them to her. Not to cover herself, but because her skin craved the warm suede of his palms. "I didn't say you had to remove them." Her voice was so husky she hardly recognized it as her own.

Rab opened his eyes, and the heat they contained could have ignited kindling. "Helen."

Her name on his lips made her shiver with pleasure. She was throbbing again and tired of waiting. She wanted this. "It's my turn, Rab." She tugged her bodice lower, watching in satisfaction as Rab's eyes blazed and he grunted in approval, his fingers running over her scars.

Then she sank to her knees in front of him. She wanted to explore and learn about his body. "May I touch you?"

"Helen, I . . ." His legs quivered as if in anticipation. "Always. Your touch is always welcome."

She trembled at his words and placed her hands on his thighs, gliding them up his legs against the natural grain of his fur, the strands tickling as they slid through her fingers.

"But you don't have to. I'm not built the same . . ." He trailed off on a groan as her hands stopped at the juncture of his legs.

She stroked the coarser outer fur and marveled at how much softer it became between his legs. Her hands met a prominent bulge, and she traced her finger along the sides. "Tell me what I'm touching."

"My sheath," he grunted.

"This is your dick?" Helen couldn't imagine how this would work if he was covered with fur, but she wanted him bad enough to give it a try.

"Yes. No. I mean, my dick is inside the sheath. Fuck, Helen," he groaned. "That feels so good. I'm about to drop."

While unsure what that meant, she suspected it was exactly what she wanted to happen. She arched her back to give Rab a better view of her breasts propped on top of the bodice, then worked her hands along his sheath.

His eyelids lowered, and he ran his fingertips along the swell of her breasts, rolling one of her nipples between his thumb and forefinger. Pleasure shot straight to her core.

She applied more pressure as she rubbed her hands along his sheath, spurred on by his apparent enjoyment as much as by her curiosity about his body. She wanted to learn everything about Rab.

A moment later, his dick emerged. A darker blue than the rest of his skin, it bobbed enticingly in front of her face. *Hmmm.* Similar in shape to a human's, it had a bulbous head and a prominent vein along its length. But Rab's erection was wider and longer than any she'd seen. She traced the vein with her tongue, then took the crown into her mouth while wrapping her hands around his pulsing shaft. His silky, hot length filled her mouth with a warm spicy flavor, and her insides fluttered with need.

As she swirled her tongue around his tip and her hands worked his length, the door rattled.

Rab leaned over her, slamming the door shut with one of his palms. "Occupied," he ground out then gave a head-to-toe shudder. His free hand cupped the back of her head. He whispered her name in a tone of pure wonder.

Helen could relate. How had she gotten so lucky? She didn't normally enjoy giving head. But she wanted this. Craved Rab's salty taste. She took him as deep as she could and reveled in the response of his large body to her ministrations. While cupping his ball sack in one hand she, reached around with the other to grab his ass and pull him closer.

She bobbed her head, her motions quickening as she became increasingly turned on by his growing hardness. His muscles tightened with each stroke as he seemingly resisted the impulse to thrust hard into her mouth, letting her take the lead.

"Gods, Helen." Rab's voice had grown hoarse.

His balls tightened under her rolling fingers, and she moved both hands back to the soft skin of his shaft, encircling his girth as she swirled her tongue over the tip.

Up and down she worked him until Rab started to pull away. "I'm going to come."

She continued to suck and gripped his ass again. No way would she let him get away. Not this time. He shuddered, grunted, and thrust forward, filling her mouth with hot liquid. She swallowed, then eased her grip before softly licking the tip of his dick.

Rab panted hard above her. He let out a long, gusty breath before moving his hands to her shoulders, urging her to stand. He peered into her face. His mouth opened, then closed.

Someone banged on the door. "Outta my room, man."

"That was—"

"I know." She glanced down. His dick was still semi-erect and outside his sheath. "You need a cover." Her eyes searched the room. Someone had discarded a pink tutu on the bed. She grabbed it. "Put this on. You're now a Wookiee ballerina."

She helped Rab into the tutu as another bang sounded at the door. Rab pulled Helen to his side. "We need to talk, but later. You ready to go back out?"

She nodded as he linked his fingers with hers

and led her from the room, completely ignoring the irate guy at the door. "Let's see if there are any momos left." He guided her toward Tseten in his hand-knit, horned, Viking hat.

But Helen's mind—and heart, she feared—remained focused on the yeti who wrapped his arm around her shoulders as they moved through the crowd. She was leaving in a week, and she and Rab desperately needed to talk. He'd turned her world upside down, and she had no regrets. Well, except one . . .

They still hadn't kissed.

CHAPTER TWELVE

R ab had heard the term "third wheel" but hadn't fully appreciated what it meant until now. He tried not to scowl at Dale from across the table in Toklat Lodge's dining room.

Rab had finally realized what an idiot he'd been to distance himself from Helen, and he didn't want to waste any more time. He only had a week to convince her that they could have a future together.

Between the late-night party and visiting with Tseten, the Mountain High crew, and Dale, Rab and Helen hadn't had a moment of privacy. Rab calmed himself. Dale would be gone soon enough. Then they'd make good use of the time they had left.

As Rab filled Helen's coffee mug, like he did

every morning at the lodge, he asked, "How'd you sleep, Dale?"

"Comfy as a burrow full of fox kits?" Helen suggested, smiling at Rab over her mug. His heart did a little flip-flop. *Could she be more perfect?* He loved that she'd learned his morning greetings.

Dale let out a chortle. "That's a new one."

"It's something Rab says. Every morning, he compares his night's sleep to an Alaska animal."

Dale slurped at his coffee. "The softer side of the big yeti."

Helen shrugged. "Rab is multifaceted."

What did that mean? Was it good?

Dale leaned back in his chair. "I slept great . . . better than a baby fox." He whistled and gestured with his mug. "The Hunter Suite is mighty fine."

It was. They all were. But since it was also between the Denali and Foraker Suites, Rab hadn't felt comfortable knocking on Helen's door to pick up where they'd left off at the party—which had been thirty-six hours ago. Rab was counting. The day after the party, as soon as Tseten's group left, Dale flew Rab and Helen back to the lodge. Then poor weather grounded him for the night.

"More coffee, Dale?" Rab asked.

"Oh, no thanks. Only one cup for me each morning."

Helen's foot brushed Rab's leg under the table, as if she knew he was thinking about her. She ran her toe up his calf while casually cradling her coffee mug, as if they weren't engaged in an active game of footsy under the table.

He bit back a grin of satisfaction. Maybe she was as bad off as he was. He strangled a groan as her toe continued to inch suggestively up his leg.

Meanwhile, Dale sat across from them, completely unaware of . . . whatever was going on. He took a sip of coffee. "Weather seems to have let up this morning."

They all turned to take in the silhouette of the Alaska Range in the late morning twilight. Mercury and a few scattered stars dotted the sky.

Rab wanted to rub his hands together. Excellent. Dale would be out of here as soon as he had enough light.

Then Rab would kiss Helen. Why hadn't they kissed yet? He ached to touch her soft lips with his. First he'd kiss her slow and deep then fast and urgent, their tongues twining as passion built between them. He wanted to kiss her fully clothed and totally naked. He longed to feel her smooth skin against his fur. They could do it on the couch, in his bed, or—*fuck*—in the hot tub.

"Leave today?"

The alarm in Helen's voice snapped Rab out of his daydream.

Dale drank the last of his coffee before answering. "That's right. The ten-day forecast doesn't look good, and I may not be able to return to get you in time. You'll miss your flight back to Portland."

A pulse of panic shot through Rab. It was something he rarely felt. He was surefooted on ice, rock, and snow. His fur coat kept him warm in all conditions. And other wild animals in these parts were no match for him. But the idea of Helen leaving today made his heart race in fear, and he gripped his teacup so tightly it shattered.

Dale leaped up and rushed to the kitchen to grab a towel as Helen moved bowls out of the way of the spreading liquid.

Rab didn't care about the tea or the broken china. As soon as Dale was out of earshot, he whispered, "You're leaving?"

"I-I . . ."

He held her gaze but couldn't read her emotions.

Dale hurried back with a towel and began

soaking up the puddle spreading across the table. "Here we go." He nodded to Rab. "Hurt yourself?"

His focus fixed on Helen, Rab automatically said, "No."

"But you're bleeding."

He glanced at his hand. He'd sliced a finger and his palm. Blood oozed from the cuts, but he didn't feel a thing. Not in his hand anyway.

Helen gave him a startled look. "Here," she said as she wrapped her cloth napkin around his hand. "Put pressure on it to stop the bleeding." She pressed her hand to the cloth, her eyes no longer meeting Rab's.

She's leaving. Boarding a plane and flying right out of his life.

He stood, his chair scraping loudly against the floor. "I should see to this," he said, lifting his wounded hand. The table was a mess. Dale and Helen mopped up the tea and picked up broken china. "I can clean up," Rab said, his chest tightening, "after you two leave."

He didn't feel his hand, only his heart. Why had he let himself get so close to Helen? Yes, he'd been lonely. He couldn't deny it, nor that she was the only person he'd ever wanted to ease his loneliness. She was different, and he'd let himself wonder what it would be like to not always be on the move, dodging tourists and monster hunters. He let himself imagine settling down and spending his life with someone. With Helen.

But he was a yeti. And some yeti didn't put down roots. Any notions he'd had to the contrary were his own foolishness.

Rab rushed from the room without looking back. If Helen's face wasn't as pained as his, he didn't want to see it. Didn't want that vision of her to linger in his mind's eye after she was gone.

HELEN BLINDLY TOSSED her belongings into her bags, not caring if dirty clothes mixed with clean.

This isn't fair. She and Rab were supposed to have several days of bliss before she had to leave. Helen had planned it all out—how she would tackle him and smother him in kisses as soon as Dale left. She'd even swiped condoms from the bathroom at the Halloween party. She wanted this with Rab. Badly. Helen was ready for her yeti.

But he'd walked away. Again. And they still hadn't talked.

She had a job to return to—a life. Well, she didn't

have much of a life. But she did have a job that provided health insurance, and paid the bills and her student loans, which was important. She couldn't up and quit. Besides, what if she stayed? Rab admitted he was a wanderer. The lodge caretaker gig was only for winter.

None of this was permanent.

The room blurred as tears overflowed. This sucked. How had she let herself grow so close to him? She'd learned this lesson with her ex. That's why she'd ventured to Alaska for a month alone in the wilderness.

But she'd been far from alone. Her time with Rab at Toklat Lodge was the fullest her life had ever been.

She zipped her bags and surveyed the spacious room. No stray socks or abandoned hair ties. No more delays. It was time to face Rab.

He wasn't in his room. The first aid kit sat on the bathroom counter, gauze wrappers in the trash, the bloody napkin soaking in the sink. But no yeti.

Helen found Dale by the front door. "Have you seen Rab?"

Dale lifted his chin. "He's blowing snow from the drive." Helen hadn't even noticed the sound of the motor. "Your bags packed?" he asked. "I'll take them out."

She stood there, unable to speak. She wanted to spill her guts about Rab. But Dale had seemed oblivious to what was going on between her and Rab. And she wasn't sure she wanted to admit to Dale that she had romantic feelings for the yeti. Besides, Dale wouldn't be anyone's first choice for relationship advice. For small engine issues, he was your guy. Impending heartbreak, not so much.

This was happening too fast. She needed to say goodbye to Rab—a proper goodbye. Not a rushed wave out in the snow as Dale tossed her bags into a waiting airplane.

Dale gestured toward the sky. "Looks like this is our window. Clouds are already coming in over the mountains. The next storm system is moving in."

The wretched storm system. She had a bone to pick with Mother Nature for shortening her time with Rab. Helen glanced down at her bags. After snagging the muscle roller from a front pouch, she called, "I'll be right out."

She marched up to Rab's room to leave him a note. It wasn't the timing or the goodbye she wanted, but it was the hand life had dealt her. Another round of crap.

CHAPTER THIRTEEN

The thought of never seeing Helen again made Rab's chest ache. He'd never experienced an emotional goodbye. Was this how bull moose felt when they didn't win the cow? Or a tundra swan when they lost their mate?

Not knowing what to say to Helen or how to ease the pain, he turned to the snowblower and applied himself to a routine task. He pushed the blower blindly around the lodge grounds, a flurry of white powder filling his vision until Dale's plane took off. Then he killed the motor and watched the plane's silhouette disappear over the horizon, eyes watering with the effort not to blink as Helen flew out of his life.

He thought the pain would disappear once Helen was gone. Instead, it intensified.

Rab dropped to his knees and keened for the first time ever—a deep, throaty, yeti keen. The kind spoken of in legend. When carried on the wind, the eerie sound spawned cautionary tales to frighten children into staying safe and indoors at night.

Rab keened until his throat became sore and the newly falling snow dampened the sound of his cries. Eventually, he stumbled back into the lodge. He'd likely lost his voice—not that it mattered since he didn't have anyone to talk to.

He trudged to his room, wanting nothing more than the oblivion of sleep. Instead, he found Helen's foam roller and a note on his bed. His gut clenched like he'd taken a headbutt from a mountain goat.

Rab,

I can't tell you how much the last few weeks have meant to me. You once said you try to blend in, to be forgettable. But to me, you are unforgettable. All my best,

Helen

P.S. You can stash the muscle roller away for your use next winter. *smiley face*

He shouldn't have avoided saying goodbye.

Rab took the note and the roller across the hall to

the Denali Suite and collapsed on Helen's rumpled bed. He buried his face in her pillow, inhaling her scent—fresh tundra and something sweet and unique to her—until he fell asleep.

Nearly a week passed, and Helen's scent became a form of torture. Rab forced himself to stop sleeping in her bed and wash her bedding.

Back in the Foraker Suite, he stood in front of the sketch of himself and the old photo of her. He kissed his finger and pressed it to her one last time before lifting the frame and turning it around.

HELEN PACED the short length of her hotel bed. She'd been stuck in Fairbanks for almost a week—too many days of cold lonely walks and cramped yoga in her room, waiting for her flight to Portland.

This was supposed to have been The Month of Helen. And after nearly four weeks in Alaska, she could successfully clear her mind for a few minutes while meditating and hold a tree pose with her eyes closed. But her emotional equilibrium was less stable than when she'd arrived. She wanted to be back at the lodge with Rab.

Her goal had been to return to her life in Portland more energized, clear headed—a new Helen. To start over again in a new apartment, with a fresh perspective, both at work and in life. The new Helen would exude so much self-confidence, her friends wouldn't feel the need to give her unsolicited updates about her ex, waiting with pained faces for her reaction.

None of them would understand Rab—not that she could tell anyone about him.

Helen collapsed on the bed. It hurt to think about him, so she focused on herself again. She would examine her life choices. Where had she gotten off track?

She'd had goals. She'd gone to law school and received her degree, intending to return to Alaska to take the bar and join a practice. But then she'd met her ex and chose to stay with him in Oregon.

She rolled onto her side and clutched a pillow to her chest. Dread pooled in her stomach at the thought of returning to Portland, to the same old projects at work, the same old friends judging her.

But did she have to return?

She wanted to take control of her life, make better choices, and trust herself. When it came to her own best interests, her own happiness . . . She was an adult and fully capable of making her own decisions, regardless of what her friends and family thought was best for her.

What if she didn't go home? What if she stayed? There were law firms in Alaska. Rab was in Alaska. Being in Alaska made her happy.

Being with Rab makes me happy.

She sat up and pulled back the curtains. The weather in Fairbanks often differed from the weather around Toklat Lodge, but the Alaska Range was visible, so they weren't socked in. What was Rab doing right now? Cooking on the grill? Reading a book in front of the fire? She smiled fondly at the mental image, and warmth and yearning filled her heart.

Dale could fly her back to the lodge. Helen would be able to job search over winter. The lodge was remote, but she'd network, maybe reach out to the yeti-friendly law firm in Anchorage, Creer and Associates.

Her heart hammered with excited anticipation. This might be the change she needed. And it would mean she could return to Rab.

But did he want her? He'd been hard to read. And the way he'd ignored her when she left . . .? She didn't want to get her hopes up. Yeah, they'd enjoyed each other's company and messed around, but Rab had been distant those last few days.

If he wasn't happy to see her, she'd figure something else out. Like he said when she arrived, the lodge was big. Avoiding one another wouldn't be hard if they didn't want to spend time together. Or she'd find somewhere else to live.

Helen immediately picked up her phone, made calls, and sent emails. She got a refund for her flight, put in her notice at work, and paid for her storage unit through next spring. With every box she checked, the weight on her shoulders lifted, and she knew she'd made the right decision. Even if Rab rejected her, Alaska was home for Helen.

Her mother was the most encouraging. She cried, but not out of disappointment. She was overjoyed that Helen had decided to return home to Alaska for good.

Then Helen called Dale to arrange a flight with him in the morning.

"You got along well with Rab, I take it," Dale said.

No point in denying it. "I did. I like him a lot." Maybe too much. He might not reciprocate her feelings. But she wouldn't let her fear stop her from taking this chance.

"Glad to hear it, sunshine. He's been alone too long."

Helen next arranged for a ride to the grocery store. She needed to stock up on olives. If Rab wasn't excited to see her, olives would be her peace offering. And if he was glad, she wouldn't be averse to sucking them off the yeti's fingers.

CHAPTER FOURTEEN

R ab woke midmorning with a leaden heart. The sky was clear, and a brilliant salmon-colored glow surrounded the peaks of the Alaska Range. Helen would have loved it. But she wasn't even in Alaska anymore. Her flight had left in the middle of the night.

He'd stayed up, watching for the flashing jet lights in the sky, as if he might see her plane crossing the Alaska Range on her flight south.

Now that she was truly gone, Rab tried to get on with his usual enjoyment of Toklat Lodge. But it had lost its charm. Ridiculous, since it was no different than last week or last winter. It had a kitchen full of tasty food, a library of books to read, cozy beds with silky sheets, a hot tub, and priceless views. Things he'd loved for years.

But Rab had experienced what the lodge could be, what life could be, with Helen by his side. Without her, everything was dull.

Rab stared down at his plain oatmeal. He couldn't be bothered to add anything to it. The unappetizing beige glop reflected his general attitude at the moment.

He washed down a tasteless, gluey mouthful with tea. On a sigh, Rab stretched out his legs and stared at the mountains. He had another long day in front of him, even after sleeping in. The sun had nearly crested the peaks, which put the time closer to lunch than breakfast. Not that it mattered. Being alone meant he could sleep all day and stay up all night if he wanted.

He'd just forced down another spoonful of oatmeal when he heard the far-off drone of an airplane engine. Dale didn't come out very often, but it made sense that he'd want to check on the lodge after the storm. Maybe Rab should get a satellite communicator. He could message Dale that everything was fine. Heck, he'd be able to check in each fall to let Dale know when he planned to arrive for winter.

He could also contact Helen . . .

No. Some things were better left alone. Rab's relationship with her was one of those things. He needed to leave behind the magical time with Helen and move on.

Rab cleared his breakfast and did the dishes as the plane landed. It took longer than usual since he needed to keep the bandages on his right hand dry. He didn't have dishwashing gloves. They probably didn't make them in his size anyway.

Dale might be a one-cup-of-coffee kind of guy, but he'd still want that one cup. Rab started a pot. But the coffee had barely begun to drip when the plane engine roared again as if for takeoff.

That was odd.

Worried it might be strangers, Rab quickly dried his hands and used the side door to check it out. If it wasn't Dale's plane, he'd fade into the background—unless someone needed him for an emergency.

Rab squinted in confusion. The aircraft had all the markings of Dale's plane. He watched it taxi then lift off.

His focus shifted to a lone figure standing at the end of the drive. Long dark hair swirling in the wind as she bent to pick up her bags.

Rab's heart lurched into overdrive.

Helen.

He took one step toward her and another. Then Rab ran. He wanted to pick her up. Crush her to his chest. Kiss her in all the ways he'd imagined.

He stopped a foot away from her. "Helen." Her name fell from his lips like the answer to a prayer. "You're back."

She nodded, her cheeks rosy from the cold. "I hope it's okay."

Okay? Okay? It was fucking awesome. He stepped forward. "Yes, I . . ." Words couldn't get past a swell of emotion. He wanted to tell her he'd fallen hard for her. That life felt broken without her. That the sun hadn't risen since the last time he'd seen her.

He cleared his throat and tried again. "It's more than okay." Rab took her gloved hand. "I'm not sure why you're back. But I need to say what I should have said before you left. I like you, Helen. Like, really like you. We should have talked after we messed around. But everything happened so fast. I didn't want to hold you back. You have a life outside of this lodge, outside of Alaska. I've lived a full life even within my limited options. And everything I've done has been on my own, alone."

Helen's breath hitched, and her face fell.

He clutched her hand tighter. "I didn't mind it until I met you. But I'm tired of being alone." He swallowed, nerves churning the oatmeal and tea in his stomach. "I don't want to be alone anymore. I don't want a life without you. That is, if you want to give us a try."

There. He'd said it. Rab held his breath and hoped Helen felt the same.

***

HELEN'S INSIDES WERE UNSETTLED, and not only because of the turbulent flight. She was reeling from the sight of Rab running toward her like in some cheesy romance, but through a field of snow instead of flowers. It left her squeeing inside.

She'd planned this moment. She'd declare her intentions, say her piece, and Rab would finally have to open up to her. But he beat her to it. And when he mentioned living his life alone, her heart froze with fear that he'd want to continue to live that way.

But thank god he didn't because Helen needed Rab like, like . . . oatmeal needed toppings.

"First," she began, "you should know that I came

back here for *me*. I've spent too many years trying to please other people. My intention isn't to be selfish but to recognize my own needs and stop putting myself second all the time. Like on an airplane when they tell you to put your own oxygen mask on before helping others."

Rab looked at her blankly. "Dale never says that." Then he smiled, a pleased, encouraging smile. "But I think I understand. If you are unwell, you can't help others."

She let out a long breath. "Exactly. Until I make things right with myself, I'm going to fail with others."

He scowled. "If you're talking about your ex, he's a diseased porcupine with dull quills."

This yeti and his sayings. "Was he?" She asked, amused but taking his meaning seriously. "He shouldn't have broken off the relationship the way he did, but maybe he left because I was unhappy, and that made him unhappy."

Blue fingers reached out and cupped Helen's cheek. "What makes you happy?"

"Alaska," she said, then closed her eyes and sighed as she leaned her face into his hand. "And you."

She didn't hear Rab move, but he was suddenly so close she felt the heat of his body.

His hand moved from her cheek to her waist before lifting her, wrapping his arms around her middle, crushing her against him.

Eye to eye now, it was her turn to reach out and stroke his face. To touch his velvety blue skin and downy white fur.

Her fingertips glided across his lips, and his eyelids lowered in response. He moaned and whispered, "Helen."

Then, finally, those big blue lips were on hers, sliding, pulling, sucking—warm and delicious. She tentatively traced his lower lip with her tongue, and Rab growled, clutching her tighter against him. His tongue met hers, the rough contrast to her own sent thrills through her body, and she wrapped her legs around his middle. Rab's kiss did not disappoint. It was everything she'd imagined—so good, so right. So freakin' hot.

A gust of wind made them come up for air, chests heaving and foreheads pressed together. "I've wanted to do that for so long," Helen admitted.

"Not as long as I have."

Helen flushed and leaned back a fraction, cocking her head.

"I knew your name when I first saw you," he reminded her. "I've wondered about you for years, Helen. Held you in a special place in my memories. When I saw you in the hot tub, you surpassed everything I remembered and even what my imagination had filled in, and I wanted you."

She remembered the way his heated gaze on her bare chest had sent sparks to her girly bits. "I was turned on too," she confessed.

Her legs tightened around him. She wanted more than kisses from the yeti. "Rab, I . . ." What should she say? I have condoms? Can we get freaky? Is this even possible? From what she'd seen of his dick—and she'd seen, felt, and tasted every big blue inch of it—it wouldn't be a problem. "Should we take this kissing inside? Maybe to a bedroom?"

"Helen," he growled, his hands cupping her backside, his fingers kneading.

Her nipples went hard. She was wet already. "Or the couch?"

"The shower."

"The hot tub."

"The dining room table."

She let out a moan. His fingers traced the seam of her jeans where her legs spread wide around him. "It's already one of my favorite places," she murmured against his lips as she not so subtly rubbed herself against his hand.

"Hang on to me," he grunted.

Helen did as he requested. She was back at Toklat Lodge. Back with Rab. She would hang on to the yeti and never let go.

CHAPTER FIFTEEN

With Helen latched around his middle, Rab reached down and picked up her bags, one in each hand. She brushed light kisses across his face as he carried her and her things into the lodge.

It was sweet torture to have her so close and not be able to return her caresses.

They didn't make it to any of the places they'd suggested. With lips locked together, he dropped her bags inside the door. She slid down his body and, in their frenzy, they stumbled over the bags, eventually collapsing on the rug near the dying embers of last night's fire.

He tugged at her jacket. "We have too many clothes on." He needed to feel her skin against his palms, chest, legs.

"We really do." Together they unzipped, yanked, and pulled. Nimble fingers peeled off layers until, inch by inch, her bare skin finally rubbed against his fur.

She let her eyes drift shut. "You feel so good against me."

"You're so smooth, so soft." He couldn't get enough of her skin. As Rab kissed her, he slid his hands up her sides to her breasts. "You don't know how badly I've wanted to hold your tits in my hands, see them in my palms."

"I've wanted that too," she said, arching her back and pushing her breasts toward him. His fingers tightened, and she gasped in a way that made him feel like a god. He moved to her nipples, lightly rolling her hard nubs between his fingers. Then he pressed open-mouth kisses down her throat to her chest.

When his lips closed around a nipple, she moaned. "Your tongue is magical."

Rab's dick had dropped and was achingly hard, pulsing at Helen's words.

He caught the scent of her arousal. She was wet. Ready for him. He trailed a hand down the side of her body, teasing her inner thigh before sliding a finger between her folds.

She bucked in response, causing a groan to rumble out of him. She was so perfect.

He dipped his finger into her, coating it in her slickness before swirling it around her clit, making her writhe. He pinched one taut nipple while grazing his teeth over the other.

Helen gasped. "Oh god, I'm com—" Her body shook in his arms as her orgasm tore through her. Rab would never tire of watching his Helen in the throes of passion.

Breathless and still quivering, she kissed him—hard—stirring something deep within him. Rab needed to bury himself inside this woman.

Helen ended the kiss with a smack and peered intently into his eyes. "I want you, Rab." She dropped her hands from his cheeks and reached over to her discarded bag.

His heart thrummed.

She held up a condom. "Inside me," she clarified. "It'll work, right?"

Rab grabbed the condom from her, his hands shaking. "We are sexually compatible. Most yeti have some human DNA. I'm just . . ." He looked down and wrapped a hand around the considerable girth of his deep-blue dick and stroked. "Bigger than most human males." He peeked up to see her reaction. He didn't want to scare or hurt her.

But Helen's response was to kiss him again. Hard nipples raked across his chest. "I know your dick, Rab. I've wrapped my hands around it. Slid my tongue along it. And taken it so far into my mouth that it hit the back of my throat."

She had. And hearing her describe it almost made Rab come all over her chest. He groaned. Another time.

"I'm up for the challenge." She helped slide the condom on, her fingers tickling as they fluttered over his shaft and down to briefly cup his balls.

With surprising strength, Helen pushed Rab to a seated position. She straddled him and lined up his dick with her entrance.

He kissed her softly and laced his fingers with hers. Their eyes locked as she lowered herself. She was slick but tight and surrounded him like a perfect glove, her inner walls squeezing around his shaft as she eased herself downward.

When she was seated fully, he made a primal noise of satisfaction that wasn't quite human, but she didn't seem to care. "Helen, you feel so perfect."

She was perfect, and the *moment* was perfect.

He and Helen were joined, and they were about to rock each other's world.

IF HELEN COULD HAVE MADE the same gratified growl as Rab, she would have. He was big in all ways, and she had to spread her legs wide. But she'd taken him inside her—to the hilt. She'd never been this turned on and felt wild with the sensations. So full. So stretched. So incredibly aroused.

Her naked body brushed exquisitely against his fur. Like wearing a fuzzy coat inside out, except it moved, touched, pressed, and kissed. She circled her hips before slowly sliding up and down his length.

He groaned, one hand moving to her waist, the other to the nub between her legs.

She arched her neck. "Yesss." He knew just how to touch her.

They found a delicious rhythm of sliding and stroking, heightening one another's pleasure as their bodies worked together.

"This is better than in my dreams." His fingers gripped her hips as she ground into him. "And I've dreamed about this—a lot—this last month."

So had she. When her subconscious ruled, Rab

had dominated her mind and body. But her dreams paled when compared with reality.

Helen captured Rab's lower lip between her own and tugged. He leaned forward and nipped at her, his dick hitting new angles as they shifted positions. She cried out, "I'm going to come again."

She'd never had back-to-back orgasms, but of course Rab could get her there.

He cradled her back, so her body leaned away from him, then swirled his thumb around her clit again.

She clutched at him as another orgasm ripped through her. Her cries echoed in the large room's vaulted ceiling.

Rab had to be close too. His grip tightened as his thrusts quickened, growing fiercer and more determined. Intense aftershocks of pleasure shot through her with each upthrust. And having him come apart in her arms, his dick twitching inside her, left Helen so high she felt like she would never come down.

CHAPTER SIXTEEN

R ab wrapped an arm around Helen, spooning against her naked body in the middle of his California king. He'd always loved this bed, but sharing it with her brought his satisfaction to a new level.

Her fingers trailed up and down his arm. "I see why you chose this room. North- and south-facing windows."

He paused from kissing her shoulder to look up at one of the large picture windows framing the brilliant green northern lights. They danced energetically across the sky as if in celebration. He hummed appreciatively and felt her smile against his hand, which she'd tucked under the side of her face.

She sighed. "What a show."

"It's for us."

"You think?"

"Many cultures have ideas about the aurora bore-alis. I've only seen them a few times this winter . . . Then you come back, and we make love like the wildest of Alaska animals. I don't think it's a coincidence."

Rab went back to contentedly nuzzling her neck. Mother Nature had a reason for everything. Even the storm that had separated him from Helen for a week had served a purpose. She'd needed the time to sort out what she wanted. Rab hooked a leg over hers possessively. Thank god she wanted him.

Helen's hand found his hip, her fingers threading through his fur. "Rab?"

"Yeah, beautiful?" He pressed another kiss to her shoulder.

"We'll make this work, right? This is for real? I mean beyond this winter and climbing season.

A successful, long-term relationship between a human and yeti would be full of challenges, no doubt about it. "This isn't just a winter fling. This *is* real." He squeezed her close. "We'll make this work."

She was quiet. Too quiet?

"Isn't that what you want?" He brushed her hair

away from her face so he could better read her reaction.

One tear rolled down her cheek, and she sniffed. "I want it so much. These aren't sad tears." She heaved a gusty sigh and turned to bury her face into his shoulder. "I'm so happy."

"I'm happy too," he confided and found her lips. Truth was, Rab was bursting. He never knew life could be so full.

Her tongue flicked out, and he opened for her as she rolled on top of him, her legs spreading to wrap around his hips. When they broke the kiss, her hands wound around him, her body pressed against his chest. "Can we have oatmeal for breakfast in the morning?"

He smiled. "Of course. What kind?"

"Something fit for a sated human who's spent the night wrapped around a yeti in a king-size bed. Surprise me."

He rumbled a laugh and kissed her forehead. "Always."

EPILOGUE

The Following August

Wispy snowflakes drifted through the air, disappearing into the steaming water and melting when they hit Rab's thick, white fur. He relaxed against the galvanized tub with a sigh, the water soothing his calloused hands and sore muscles. Through slitted eyes, he reveled in the view before him.

Fleece-covered arms slid around to hug his neck from behind. "You're facing the wrong direction." Helen's breath tickled his ear. "The valley in all its golden, autumnal glory is behind you."

She began kneading the knots between his shoulder blades, and he groaned at the pleasure of her touch and the relief to his muscles. "I disagree. The mountains are behind clouds, and the river has always been there. Neither compares to our house, with smoke curling from the chimney and the vibrant red tundra on the hills behind it."

Helen didn't say anything, but her lips grazed his cheek before she slid her arms around him once more, squeezing him tight.

Rab still couldn't believe this beautiful, framed structure was his and Helen's. Built by their own hands with blood, sweat, and tears of joy. No more wandering the Alaska Range between jobs. Rab had put down roots—made a home—with Helen.

This fall his hands had callouses from swinging a hammer, not from scraping against rocky crags while living in the often-harsh conditions of high-altitude mountains. The rocks weren't going anywhere. When Rab felt the pull to wander and Helen didn't have to work, they could walk out their front door and disappear into the wilds.

"You're right," she said with a sigh and tilted her head to rest her temple against his. "This is the better view. It represents us."

Rab lifted a hand from the water to clasp hers. He brought it to his lips and kissed her palm before intertwining their fingers. "All done with work?"

She perched on the edge of the tub. "I have officially clocked out from Creer for a month. I'll check back in once we get satellite internet hooked up for winter at the lodge."

He regarded the small satellite dish they'd affixed to the roof of the house. They'd soon be taking it down to store for winter. All summer, Helen had juggled her new remote position with Creer and Associates and house construction, working in their temporary canvas tent during the day and helping him build their home at night.

When they took off their tool belts and peeled out of sweaty clothes for the day, they'd soak in the hot tub under the dappled rays of the midnight sun. Their homemade contraption circulated water through a metal hose they'd coiled around a fire pit. And the fire did double duty, heating the water in the coil while the smoke kept the mosquitoes at bay.

At the memory of her lithe body in the small tub, their energetic lovemaking putting out the fire and reducing the water level to half the original, he growled and tugged on her arm. "Join me."

She resisted. "Hey, you're getting me wet."

He tipped his head back to meet her gaze. "Good."

She ruffled his fur. "Not that kind of wet." But her lids lowered over smoldering eyes.

"Come on. Let's end our first summer like we started it."

She crossed her arms. "I started summer in Anchorage at Creer while our pile of construction materials sat here under two feet of snow. You were still on Denali."

He rolled his eyes. "My summer didn't begin until I met you here." Just like his life hadn't really begun before he'd met Helen. "And besides, it was a good idea to bring our materials out from the lodge by snow machine in the spring. No one could have predicted all the late-season snow."

"True." She tilted her face up to the sky, the late August snowflakes slowly wafting down—earlier than some years, though not unheard of. "But Dale could come at any time to pick us up. The second I take my shirt off, we'll hear his plane."

Rab shifted, his dick growing hard at the thought of Helen's perfect breasts, her dark nipples right at water level when she sank into the tub. "If you hear a plane, it's just Dale flying guests to and from the lodge." They were close enough to hear the occasional small aircraft, but far enough away and separated by swampy lowlands that even adventurous guest out for a hike wouldn't stumble upon them.

"He won't come here for a few weeks," Rab insisted. "Besides, he has to land on the gravel bar down by the river." He tugged gently on her hand. "You'd hear him and have plenty of time to pull a shirt on before he walked up the hill."

"Not helping," she said, but she wasn't pulling away and her lids were still lowered as she regarded the dark water where he was most definitely stiffening. She trailed her fingers through the rippling surface. "It's hot." She looked tempted.

"Join me."

"A soak would be nice."

"Especially while I rub your back."

"We may not have started our summer this way, but . . ." Her lips quirked into a sexy smile. She held her free hand out to watch the delicate snowflakes land in her palm. "I was naked in a hot tub in the falling snow when you met me."

He suppressed a groan at the memory of surprising Helen in Toklat Lodge's hot tub the year before. She'd screamed, and he'd looked away. But he'd recognized her, and the attraction was instantaneous—and mutual, thankfully. "So if you get naked now, it will be like coming full circle."

In one fluid movement, she pulled off her fleece and shirt. She wasn't wearing a bra—the tease. Her dark nipples puckered into hard peaks, and Rab licked his lips.

"I like the idea of coming full circle." Her hands were at her fly, her jeans parting to reveal the pink edge of her panties. She hooked her thumbs into the waistbands of both and pulled them down together.

She stood bare before him, causing his mouth to grow dry. No matter how many times he saw her smooth curves, he would never tire of the view, and it was the only view better than their house.

"As memorable as our meeting was," she said as she inched toward him, "I'm happy to be in *our* hot tub at *our* house."

Her words thrilled him. He'd been nervous about giving up his nomadic summers—they'd been all he'd ever known. But being here with Helen felt so right. Like he was finally home.

He lifted a wet hand toward her, and she took it. "This time," he said, his words coming out in a growl, "I intend to claim you."

She reached up, tracing her fingers along the two faint red lines above her breast where his claws had marked her. "You already have." Her voice was husky as she lifted one leg and then the other into the tub, while Rab's heart raced in anticipation.

She didn't sit across from him or nestle in his lap for her back rub. Instead, she spread her legs wide, straddling Rab's thighs and, lining up her sex with the tip of his eager dick, she lowered herself onto him. "I'm yours," she said as she sank down, taking him in. "Body and soul. Forever."

"Forever," he repeated. Rab was quite sure she'd just claimed *him*—again.

Thank you for reading Ready for Her Yeti!
Please consider leaving a review. Reviews make it easier for others to find this book.

Ready for more yeti romance? Check out Toni and Denzin's story in Fake Dating Her Yeti.

Toni never thought she would fake a relationship, but when she agrees to be her yeti boss's plus one at a Thanksgiving wedding, she risks everything, including her heart.

Subscribe to Neva's newsletter and find out how Rab and Helen celebrate next Halloween in a free bonus scene!

www.nevapostauthor.com/readyforheryeti-bonus

SNEAK PEEK OF FAKE DATING HER YETI

Toni stared at Denzin. Had he just agreed to *fake date* her? She resisted the urge to squirm in her chair, body heating under his intense steel-blue gaze.

She glanced down at the picture on her phone screen and suppressed a shudder. She wanted nothing to do with the guys her mother had chosen. *I want Denzin.* But he was her boss, technically. Off limits. Should they even pretend?

While Denzin gave her space to think, Mari didn't. "Girl, what say you?" She waggled her eyebrows adding, "Having a date for the weekend, real or not, sounds like a good time to me."

Be at Denzin's side for several days? Toni pictured him in his custom tux, broad, yeti shoulders filling out a black jacket, muscular legs and tight ass in well fitted pants. Even now with his large, blue hand wrapped around a mug of beer he radiated sexy, authoritative appeal. Back straight, trim white facial fur dusting that chiseled blue jaw, Mountain High tee-shirt appearing more formal on Denzin than anyone else. The yeti was hot.

Toni's heart thumped, telling her to do it, try it, take advantage, and get to know Zin better. Meanwhile, the worrier inside tried to slam the brakes. Fake relationships were for the movies. And pretending to date at the wedding could make things weird afterward—especially with people who didn't know the truth. She didn't want to jeopardize her professional reputation.

She scrubbed her face with her hands. She'd been living safe for so long. Too long. The likelihood of any significant consequences was remote. Maybe she should take a chance. Do something daring. It *would* be a good time—if they pulled it off.

Toni dropped her hands and regarded Denzin, his focus still on her. "Okay. I'll do it."

Full, sky-blue lips curled into a smile aimed at her. She'd been flushed before, now her internal temperature shot to approximately one thousand.

Order your copy today!

ALSO BY NEVA POST

Alaska Yeti Series:

Ready for Her Yeti

Fake Dating Her Yeti

Yeti for Love

~ *Coming soon* ~

Rescued by Her Yeti

Married to Her Yeti

Loved by Her Yeti

ACKNOWLEDGMENTS

I would never have made it this far without years of critique group support and dinners that I didn't have to cook.

A huge thank you to Elizabeth, Erin, Heather, Karen, Lynn, and Tam (yes, in alphabetical order)! I cannot thank you enough for the read throughs, advice, and encouragement. Heather and Elizabeth, I couldn't have gotten across the finish line without you. Elizabeth, you have my deep gratitude for bringing Yeti Love into the world with your monster romance challenge.

Scott, you're my cinnamon roll hero. Thank you for your patience when I spend evenings writing or plot out loud, for reading romance when it's not your thing, and for keeping us fed.

M&D, Maggie, and Leah, I greatly appreciate your input and support along the way.

ABOUT THE AUTHOR

Neva Post grew up in a log house in Interior Alaska where she walked uphill both ways to school at temperatures of negative forty with only the aurora borealis to light her way. At least, that's how she remembers it.

She's equally happy on a snowy trail or coaxing vegetables to grow in her garden during the long Alaskan summer days. When she's not waxing skis or chasing voles out of her cabbage, she's at her computer. Neva's novels include paranormal elements—she can't help it—with smart and dependable characters who always get their HEA.

www.nevapostauthor.com

facebook.com/nevapostauthor

instagram.com/nevapostauthor

Made in the USA
Columbia, SC
16 September 2024

41476719R00107